KILLER INSTINCT

KILLER INSTINCT

S. E. GREEN

SIMON PULSE   NEW YORK   LONDON   TORONTO   SYDNEY   NEW DELHI

SIMON PULSE

An imprint of Simon & Schuster Children's Publishing Division

1230 Avenue of the Americas, New York, NY 10020

First Simon Pulse hardcover edition May 2014

Text copyright © 2014 by Shannon Greenland

Front jacket, jacket spine, and case front photograph copyright © 2014 by Ada Summer/Corbis

Back jacket and back case photograph copyright © 2014 by Thinkstock

Jacket design by Jessica Handelman

All rights reserved, including the right of reproduction in whole or in part in any form.

SIMON PULSE and colophon are registered trademarks of Simon & Schuster, Inc.

For information about special discounts for bulk purchases, please contact Simon & Schuster Special Sales at 1-866-506-1949 or business@simonandschuster.com.

The Simon & Schuster Speakers Bureau can bring authors to your live event. For more information or to book an event contact the Simon & Schuster Speakers Bureau at 1-866-248-3049 or visit our website at www.simonspeakers.com.

Interior design by Mike Rosamilia

The text of this book was set in Minion Pro.

Manufactured in the United States of America

2 4 6 8 10 9 7 5 3 1

Library of Congress Cataloging-in-Publication Data

Green, S. E., 1971–

Killer instinct / S. E. Green. — First Simon Pulse hardcover edition.

p. cm.

Summary: When seventeen-year-old Lane becomes involved in the search for a serial killer active in the Washington, D.C., area, she worries that her lifelong fascination with such murderers has a very real and terrible cause.

[1. Serial murderers—Fiction. 2. Family life—Washington (D.C.)—Fiction. 3. Interpersonal relations—Fiction. 4. High schools—Fiction. 5. Schools—Fiction. 6. Criminal investigation—Fiction. 7. United States. Federal Bureau of Investigation—Fiction. 8. Washington (D.C.)—Fiction.] I. Title.

PZ7.G82632Kil 2014   [Fic]—dc23   2013037119

ISBN 978-1-4814-0285-9

ISBN 978-1-4814-0287-3 (eBook)

KILLER INSTINCT

Chapter One

I STUDY SERIAL KILLERS. THEY'RE LONERS. Obsessive-compulsives. People who lack emotion and fantasize about violence. Intelligent people who on the outside seem normal.

Interesting thing is, I fit that profile. I have urges. I plot ways to violently make people pay for what they've done to others.

Nature versus nurture. Of course I've studied that. I've got good parents with decent genetics, so for me I've always suspected it's something else. Except . . . I have no clue what.

I don't know why I am the way I am, why I think the way I think, why I do the things I do. All I know is that I'm different. Always have been. I can't remember a time when I *didn't* know something was off in me.

At ten, when other kids were coloring with crayons, I started tracking serial killers and keeping details of their murders in a journal—a journal no one has ever seen but me.

Now, nearly seven years later, most teens hang out with friends. I, however, prefer spending my spare time at the courthouse—with Judge Penn to be exact. He tries all the hard cases.

His staff expects to see me, believing my lie about wanting to go into law, and so I give my customary nod as I enter the back of Penn's court and quietly take my usual spot in the left rear corner. I sit down and get out my summer reading just in case today's calendar is boring.

It's not.

A balding, short, pudgy, accountant-type man sits beside a slick lawyer he's obviously spent a lot of money on. The Weasel is what I decide to name him.

In the viewing gallery sit a handful of women; three are crying and two stoically stare straight ahead.

On the stand is another of the expressionless ones, and she's speaking, "... classical music, a candle. He knew his way around, like he'd been in my house before. He handcuffed my ankles and wrists to the bedposts and stuffed gauze in my mouth so my screams couldn't be heard. He cut my clothes away and left me naked. He wore a condom and was clean shaven, *everywhere*. He had a full-face mask on."

No evidence.

"He raped me," she matter-of-factly reports, and then describes in detail all the vicious ways he violated her.

"I'm going to be sick," the woman in front of me whispers before getting up and leaving the room.

I continue listening to the details, mentally cataloging them. Details don't bother me. They don't make me sick. They don't make me want to leave a room. If anything they draw me in because they are just that—details, facts.

A few of the women in the room sniffle, and I glance to the Weasel. Although he's doing a good job of keeping his emotions blank, I catch a slight smirk on his lips that kicks my pulse.

This is one of the things I consider a talent of mine. While some people show every emotion, I show none. And I can read others' body language, others' faces when they think they're doing a stellar job of masking. The Weasel obviously thinks he's getting away with something.

Thirty minutes later the Weasel is found not guilty due to lack of evidence. As he walks from the court room, his slight smirk becomes more visible when he glances at one of the sniffling women.

This is another thing people make the mistake of—confidence, cockiness, ego.

The Weasel will rape again. Of this I'm sure.

If it is my destiny to be a killer, I'm going to need a type.

And today decides that my type will be criminals—specifically, those who have managed to avoid punishment.

I turn seventeen next week. The Weasel will be my birthday present to myself. I think I've just found my first victim.

Chapter Two

AS I PUSH DOWN ON THE FRENCH PRESS plunger, I glance across the kitchen counter to my fifteen-year-old younger sister. She's the quintessential "perfect" teenager. Popular, student council, flat-ironed blond hair, okay grades, cheerleader, great clothes, curvy, cute body.

These are not the reasons I dislike her. I know the *real* Daisy. Her popularity is milked from others, her blond hair is fake, her okay grades come from cheating, and she plays the I'm-your-best-friend game a little too well.

"Who makes French press every morning?" she says snidely, always showing me her true self.

I don't bother responding.

My still-sleepy eight-year-old brother shuffles in and wraps his arms around my waist. "Morning, Lane."

I give him a hug. "Morning."

Both Daisy and my brother, Justin, are half siblings to me. Although I remind myself of that fact nearly every day with Daisy, I've never once with Justin.

Justin had been labeled learning disabled early on, but looking at him you'd never know anything's wrong. There's just something not firing up there in that complicated brain of his.

I put my arm around his skinny shoulders. "You scared about starting the big team-taught classes this year?" He used to be in all small self-contained ones.

"A little," he mumbles.

"Your teachers wouldn't have recommended it if they didn't believe in you," Daisy says encouragingly.

Our mutual love of Justin is the only thing that keeps me somewhat, and I do stress the word "somewhat," okay with my sister.

Our mom clicks into the kitchen on her sensible heels. "Good morning, children!"

"That's a little too cheery for a first day of school," I joke.

She tugs on the tips of my long kinky red hair. "Love it down."

I gift her one of my rare smiles. "Thanks."

I divide the strong roast between two travel mugs and slide one across the granite counter to Mom. She grins as if I've just served up the Holy Grail on a platter, and *that* is the reason I go through the trouble of making great coffee every morning.

She gives me a peck on the cheek, then leans down to do the same to Justin. "Phew, go brush your teeth."

He breathes on her just to be ornery, and shuffles off to the bathroom.

Mom rounds the kitchen island to kiss Daisy, who does her customary avoidance by hopping off her stool and heading up to her bedroom.

This is yet another reason why Daisy tiptoes a fine line with me. Let Mom kiss you already. It won't kill you.

Pretending she's not hurt, Mom turns to me. "My first big day too." She motions to her navy suit. "Good?"

Mom works in DC at FBI headquarters. So does my stepdad, Victor. That's where they met after my dad died. Except Mom's climbed the promotions ladder a lot quicker than Victor. Her latest step up is the biggest ever. Director of the behavioral Analysis unit. They handle serial killers.

What did he do when you caught him?
How did he pick his victims?
Was there a lot of blood?
There's a video of the kill room? Can I watch it?

Mom had always patiently answered my questions as honestly as possible, writing it off as healthy kid interest. But when

I asked her that last one, I could tell it weirded her out, which is why I stopped asking questions several years ago.

"You look great, Mom. Very director."

She grabs her purse. "Dad'll be back in a few days from California, and then we'll all do a celebratory dinner."

"Sounds good."

"Justin doesn't have aikido today, but he does have after-school tutoring."

I nod. "I know."

She laughs. "Of course you know. You get your organization from me." She waves her hand around our overly neat house before opening the front door. "Later. Can't wait to hear about first days."

You get your organization from me. That puts it lightly. Mom's a bit OCD. Attention to details, combing facts, noticing the small things. It makes her very good at her job.

Dressed in my usual skinny jeans, snug tee, and gray Pumas, I grab my school stuff and head out to my Jeep Wrangler. As I wait for Daisy and Justin, my thoughts trail to the Weasel. I wonder what he's doing this very second. He's probably heading to work, like every other adult. Unlike every other adult, he's going to sit in his safe little office, think about the women he's raped, and plan the next one. Just the vision has me clenching my jaw. . . . He'll get what he deserves.

Justin and Daisy come out of the house, and I refocus my energies on driving. At the elementary campus Justin climbs out. "You're going to do great," I tell him, and he gives me that toothless grin that always tugs at my heart.

Daisy and I pull in to the high school, and she's already climbing out before I stop. In my peripheral vision I see her bound away and join her sophomore clique.

I'm in the gifted-and-talented program so most of my senior classes are in the GT wing.

"Slim," my last-year lab partner greets me as I enter the main building.

"Hey." I've been called Slim for as long as I can remember. I'm five-eight, skinny, and flat-chested. It's not like I try to be skinny. I eat normal. Mom says I get it from my real dad's side of the family.

At my locker the science club president comes up. "How's it going, Slim?"

Sometimes I wonder if people remember my name's Lane. "Good."

"Go anywhere this summer?"

I spin my combination. "Nope." Just the courthouse, but that's my little secret. Among other things . . .

He hands me a flyer. "I'm assuming you're doing science club again?"

I take the flyer. "Sure." The science club is my main attempt at socializing. Other than that I keep to myself, don't speak unless I have something notable to say, and don't care what people think. If that avoidance behavior makes me unpopular, then so be it.

"Great. We're aiming for the national plaque this year, so we can use all the smart we can get. We're looking at . . ."

His voice fades away as my thoughts trickle in. I need to go to the main office and make sure I snag the TA job for the library this year. Sure my scores are high enough, but I need extracurricular if I'm getting into UVA's Biology program.

"All right. First meeting's next Wednesday after school. See you then," he says, and heads off.

"Yeah, see you then."

I go through my first day of senior year as expected. I do indeed get the TA job. I go to all my classes with the same teachers and same students as my other years. When you're in GT, it's like that. There are no surprises. Boring's good. At least where normal life's concerned, boring's good.

I don't see my sister until it's time to leave. "I'll catch a ride home," she tells me. "We"—she motions over her shoulder to her pack of annoying friends—"are going to hang out."

I nod and don't bother reminding her Mom wants us all home by seven for dinner. If Daisy doesn't remember, it's not my problem.

Justin's in his after-school tutoring program so I head straight to the army surplus store. I need to browse supplies and brainstorm a little. I have to figure out how I'm going to deal with the Weasel.

Chapter Three

I MET MY ONLY REAL FRIEND, REGGIE, when I was eight and she ten. We shared bunk beds at a science and technology summer camp. We immediately clicked on a, let's just say, weird level. We "got" each other. We let each other be who we needed to be. We were okay to sit for an hour and not speak. We were who we were, and that was fine with both of us.

When I was ten and she twelve, we attended our usual summer camp. There was this girl who picked on everybody. She was horrible. She'd rub poison oak on girls' underwear. She'd pour acetone in shampoo bottles. She'd take pictures in the showers and pass them among the boy campers.

Pranks are okay, but hers were way too mean-spirited to qualify as pranks.

When I told Reggie that I wanted to make the girl pay, Reggie didn't blink an eye.

And when I told her *how* I intended on making her pay, Reggie said, "Want some help?" I knew then that we were soul mates.

But I didn't make Reggie help me—my thing is my thing. And when the girl showed up the next day with an oak rash on her ass, acetone burns on her scalp, *and* naked pictures all over the boys' cottages, she never messed with anyone again.

Making people pay for their dysfunctional aggression allows me to deal with my own urges. I learned that a long time ago. When I first shared that thought with Reggie, she nodded and replied, "I get that."

Reggie's from upstate New York, and summer camp was always the only time we ever saw each other. She earned a full-ride scholarship to MIT.

She's got to be the smartest person I know, and she's got her cyberfingers in everything. Thanks to her I've learned a thing or two about hacking, about covering my tracks, about using different IP addresses so things can't be traced. Of course I'm nothing at her level, but I can do basic things like get an address for Paul Dryer, otherwise known as the Weasel.

I grab my book bag. "Mom, I'm gone."

"Set the alarm when you get home," she yells from her bathroom.

There's a late-night coffeehouse a few blocks away from our house. At first I went to be alone, to study, to drink coffee. Between Daisy, Justin, and my parents, I've always found it hard to concentrate at home.

Mom respects that I need my space, and as long as I'm home by midnight, she's okay with me going to that coffeehouse.

Yes, at first I used to really go there, but over the past year I've used the time to prowl the streets. I drive the neighborhoods people avoid. I watch drug deals go down, hookers get picked up, and drunks stumble the sidewalks. I follow them . . . watch them . . . learn them . . . I absorb the fear that at first watching them caused but now only draws me in. It both puzzles and mesmerizes me.

I crave my night outings, and on more than one occasion have caught myself zoning out during the day thinking about them. Sometimes they consume me. They fulfill a part of me I've yet to figure out. I can't help but wonder that if just watching these deviants causes my blood to race through my body, what will actually taking one of them down do to me?

That last thought rolls around in my brain as I drive my Wrangler straight to the Weasel's address and park across the street. In the one spot not illuminated by a streetlamp, I get out my binoculars and zero in on his third-floor condo. Immediately I pull back.

The man's not shy at all.

Naked, he strolls around his condo brushing his teeth and then talking on the phone. He gets done with that and goes on to ironing. Personally, I don't care for being naked. I prefer clothes. Nakedness is too . . . unhygienic for my taste.

Time passes and he eventually dresses in khakis and a polo. He grabs his keys and leaves his condo. Minutes after that he strolls out the complex's front door and, whistling, heads down the street.

My heart kicks in as I watch where he's going, and it only makes me more excited for how the night will play out. He can't be going far—he's on foot.

From my Jeep I watch him head a couple blocks down and straight into a restaurant. I climb out and follow the same sidewalk path until I'm standing outside the door he just went through. I step to the right and peer through the glass into the full restaurant. I inhale some fortifying air, grab the handle, and step inside.

It's packed, and no one really notices him sitting at the bar and sipping a white wine.

I remember hearing Victor say that a white wine was a sissy drink. I suppose that's why the Weasel's ordered it—to make himself look mild.

There's a ton of people waiting for a table, so I merge with the group, standing along the wall, making it look like I'm waiting too. It's a good thing this place is not just a bar, otherwise I would've already been carded and asked to leave.

Despite the fact it's September and still warm outside, the manager has the heat on inside the restaurant. I prefer cold. Always have. My core body temperature runs hot.

It doesn't take but a few minutes for a woman to approach the Weasel. I can't hear what he's saying, but he's got the I'm-just-an-awkward-nerd routine down a little too well. And the woman is falling for it, big time—just like all the other women did. She's probably ten years younger than him and too stupid to realize he really isn't drunk.

Pity lays are what they give him. Or at least what they *think* they're going to give him.

The thing about the Weasel is that he doesn't have a type. The women in the courtroom had been tall/short, chunky/skinny, blonde/brunette.

This one wears her black hair short and displays big boobs that definitely don't look fake.

"Miss?" The hostess waves at me. "Table?"

I snap out of my staring. "I'm waiting for someone." I check my watch to make it look true.

"It's going to be an hour wait at this point. Want to go ahead and put your name in?"

"No, thank you."

She gives me a polite smile and goes back to hostessing. I go back to staring.

The Weasel and Big Boobs progress in the get-to-know-you-drunk thing, and sometime later they stumble from the restaurant—her really wasted and him faking it. I see her pass him a car key. They're going somewhere not on foot.

It didn't occur to me they would drive, and so as normal as I can make it seem, I head from the restaurant, jog the couple blocks back to my Jeep, and hope they are still there when I return.

They are, leaning up against her car out front, making out. I watch, a little disgusted at their sloppy display, waiting for them to make the next move.

He pulls away from their groping and climbs into her car to drive. Twenty minutes later they arrive at a Cape Cod. They go inside and I know, based on what I heard in the courtroom, how it goes from here. She wants it, the Weasel refuses (as he did with all the other women), choosing instead *talking*. The talking I'm sure convinces the women he's harmless.

An hour later he finally emerges. He walks the perimeter of her house before heading from the neighborhood, getting into a cab, and pulling away. Miss Big Boobs will be his next victim—this I'm sure. I hope I'll be there to take him down.

Chapter Four

I SPEND THE NEXT UNEVENTFUL COUPLE of days going to school, doing my normal routine, and eagerly thinking about the Weasel. Each night I spy on him as he does his naked routine in his third-floor condo, and I fantasize about how I'm going to make him suffer.

On the third night I park in my usual spot, get out my binoculars, and see him naked, standing in his bathroom, meticulously shaving his face, arms, chest, legs, and pubes.

No evidence.

Tonight will be the night. My whole body vibrates in expectation.

While he continues his ritual, I start my own with the supplies I bought from the surplus store and the one I stole. . . .

I stuff my springy red hair into a full-face ski mask, slip my leather gloves on, and tuck my long-sleeve dark tee into my black cargo pants.

No evidence.

Into those cargo pockets I put a Taser, the stolen tranquilizer gun, zip ties, and my lock pick. This is my first time and my personal kit will likely change as I fine-tune my methods. I recognize this and am looking forward to that evolution.

The Weasel drives from the underground garage in his perfectly normal Corolla and pulls right past me.

I don't immediately follow. I know where he's headed—the Cape Cod and Miss Big Boobs.

About twenty minutes later I pull onto her street and right past the Weasel's Corolla. He's already gone inside.

I park in the darkness under a tree and cut my engine. I lower the face portion of my mask and take a second to calm my anticipatory nerves. This is it. The night I become me. The start of everything. In my mind it goes two ways: Either I kill him. Or I don't kill him.

If I kill him, he deserves it for how he raped all those women. If I don't kill him, I'll make him suffer, and I'll enjoy every minute of it. It'll curb the urges I have lived with for years and have only mildly satiated. Tonight is the night I completely fulfill that dark, missing side of me that has persistently been clawing at my insides. I want to do this. I *have* to do this.

When I feel ready, I climb from the Jeep and stay to the shadows as I approach the house. At eleven in the evening no one's out in the sleepy, family neighborhood.

I skirt along the side yard and make my way to the back door.

Years ago Victor taught me how to pick a lock. It was all for fun, of course. He had no clue I'd really be using the skill.

He also taught me how to shoot.

I crouch at the back-porch door, fumble with the pick, and accidentally drop it through the wooden slats beneath my feet. *Dammit.*

I step down and scramble through dirt and leaves, looking for my pick. *I'm such an idiot. I can't believe I dropped the pick.* I push aside more leaves. *Where is it? There!* Its silver glints a teeny bit in the moonlight, and I reach for it, noting my hands are shaking. *No, no shaking hands. Be calm.*

I pick it up and fist it tight to not only force my hands to stop trembling but also to ensure I don't drop it again. Next time I'll pack two.

I crawl back up onto the porch and concentrate on a steady hand as I try again. The lock makes a silent *click*, and beneath my mask I smile.

I step over the threshold, silently close the door, and immediately hear classical piano. I give myself a second to orient and slowly head toward the music. Halfway down the hall, I stop, close my eyes, and blow out a very—long—calming—breath.

My eyes snap open, and I focus on candlelight flickering from a room just ahead. A vanilla scent wafts through my senses. As I draw closer, I hear whimpering and the sound of clanking metal. The two combined mute the throb in my ears and have me stepping through the doorway.

The Weasel stands in a shirt and boxers, with a face mask of his own and his pecker hanging out. The woman lies naked and handcuffed to the bed, gauze shoved in her mouth.

She sees me and immediately starts thrashing.

The Weasel turns, and through the face mask he wears I see his eyes widen.

This is it echoes across my mind, but I don't move. The Weasel seems confused for a second, then quickly snaps back to reality and makes an awkward lunge for me. I clumsily dodge away. *Face your attacker.* My sensei's words float through my brain. I'm doing everything wrong. I'm in the opposite direction!

I redirect and go toward him, blunder with the snap on my cargo pocket, and yank out my Taser. He tackles me to the floor. *Umph!* All the air leaves my lungs, and somewhere in the back of my mind I think, *I should've had the Taser out and ready.*

We roll a few times across the floor, our panting breaths filling the air. He lands on top of me and reaches for the Taser at the exact second I remember my death grip on it. I raise it up, point it toward his back, and hope to God it doesn't hit me, too. I squeeze the trigger, barbs fly out, and his whole body arches away from me.

That was close. *Too* close.

With a grunt, I shove him off me and scramble to my feet. My heart kicks into overdrive as I watch his full body spasm and listen to his shrieks. *Slim justice.*

I take in the barbs suctioned to his butt and lower back and experience a moment of both gladness that I hit him and disappointment that it wasn't his pecker I pinged. I'll have to practice my aim.

Before the .3 joules runs its course, I turn his short pudgy body over onto his stomach, and like I've seen cops do on TV, I use zip ties to secure his wrists, thighs, and ankles. I pull extra tight. Probably too tight, but I don't care. So what if his extremities experience blood loss.

I pick up the Taser and give him another jolt just to see him spasm, just to hear him yell, and to surge the blood through my veins again. His limp pecker catches my eye, and pure adrenaline spikes every nerve in my body as a new thought springs to life.

On the bedside table lies a butcher knife he would have used to intimidate and torture his latest victim. I walk over to it, pick it up, and its large blade catches the light of the flickering candles. Holding it in front of me, I slowly stalk back across the bedroom to his hog-tied form.

He sees me coming, and his body begins violently shaking with the fear he more than deserves to feel. I wave the blade in front of his face, and he whimpers like the pathetic rapist that he is. The snivels roll through my body, fueling it with a desire for righteousness.

"P-p-please don't," he begs.

Please don't what? Do to you what you've done to so many others? Make you pay for your disgusting self? Assure no one else will ever suffer by you again?

He responds to my silence with a high-pitched wail that heats my core to near boiling. With one last wave of the blade, I run it up his bare shaved thigh and draw a stream of blood. He screams even louder, before falling completely silent as realization dawns that I left his precious pecker alone. But as soon as that sinks in, he starts screaming again.

I yank his mask off and cram it in his mouth, and he goes blessedly mute.

The woman's thrashing body has my attention swerving over to the bed. I disengage the Taser cartridge and go to her. Crying and whimpering, she stares wide-eyed at me.

I cover her naked body with a blanket and pull the gauze from her mouth.

"Please," she croaks. "Please help me."

I look around the room. I had thought about this part really well—how to help her and stay anonymous at the same time. I take the phone off the bedside table and lay it right beside her head.

"Please"—she jerks at her restraints—"are you sure he's secure?"

I nod as I dial 911. The sound of the operator answering shoots realization through me. *I have to get out of here.* I bolt from the scene, through her house, across her yard, and back to my Jeep.

She'll be okay. Help will come soon.

I climb into my Wrangler, take my ski mask off, and shove it in my glove compartment. The Weasel's blood catches my eye. *Shit.*

Shit. Shit. Shit.

It's on my glove compartment, my clothes, my door handle, and anything I touched with my gloved hands. I messed up. Big time. I'm such an imbecile. I'll have to be more careful, more alert, more organized next time. No fumbling, no awkward dodging, no leftover blood. I need to have it all figured out. It has to be cleaner. Premeditated.

Okay, think. It's eleven forty-five, and I have to be home in fifteen minutes. I have a change of clothes, and I have a first aid kit with alcohol wipes. I'll shove my blood-streaked clothes in a plastic bag and immediately wash them when I get home. I'll wipe my Jeep down with alcohol and then wash it tomorrow and detail the inside. No one will know anything.

Quickly I change, and as I'm slipping out of my cargo pants, my fingers brush the tranquilizer gun still in my pocket, loaded with enough stolen sedative to destroy a man three times the Weasel's size.

I didn't kill him after all. . . .

Chapter Five

TWO MORNINGS LATER I'M IN THE KITCHEN, and the Weasel is all over the news. Just the thought of tasering him and helping that woman fills me with a craving to do it all over again.

Yes, he's all over the news, as is the Masked Savior.

Masked Savior? You've got to be kidding me.

"Ugh, that's awful," my sister groans. "That man raping those women. God, Lane, why are you watching that? Turn the channel."

I give my sister a look. What's the big deal? It's just the news.

Daisy rolls her eyes. "Don't you feel *anything*?"

I grab the remote and turn the channel. I'm not as unfeeling as people think. I show sympathy where it's warranted. I show hatred to those who deserve it. I just don't have emotions over the usual things, and to me that has its advantages. Why am I the only one who appreciates this?

"And while we're on the subject of emotions, would it kill you to laugh? In fact, I don't think I have *ever* heard you laugh."

I suppose I *should* try laughing sometime . . .

"And talking. Sometimes you're so quiet it's creepy."

. . . and talking, too. Both are very normal things. And with so many abnormal thoughts, I suppose it would behoove me to try "normal" more often. But what does that mean exactly—like Daisy and half the other teens at my school? No, "normal" is subjective, not objective. After all, I'm normal in *my* private world.

"What's creepy?" Victor says, swinging into the kitchen.

"Lane is. I told her she needs to laugh and talk more."

He pinches my cheek. "Don't listen to Daisy. You're fine just the way you are."

"Thanks."

Daisy gives a dramatic sigh. "Whatever."

"Whatever," he mimics, and Daisy giggles.

I used to make her giggle like that by arranging licorice into a hangman's noose. Sometimes I wonder if she remembers that.

Mom comes in behind me and grabs her mug of dark roast. "Did you all hear about the Masked Savior?" She laughs. "Nothing like a good vigilante."

Victor delivers a one-armed hug to me and a smooch to Mom, then rounds the island to Daisy. She willingly accepts his good-bye kiss.

Although Mom's never said so, I know it bothers her.

Mom pulls bacon from the fridge, as she does every weekend, and starts frying it up. Its deliciousness immediately fills the air. Mom has this way of cooking bacon, slow and on low heat. It takes forever but is so worth it.

As if on cue Justin shuffles downstairs. He pours himself a glass of chocolate milk and curls up on the couch to watch cartoons. "Did Dad already go golfing?"

"Just left." Mom turns to me. "You working today?"

I nod. "I'll head out after breakfast." I work nearly every Saturday as a vet tech.

Daisy's phone chimes with a text. She quickly checks it. "Mom, can I go to Samantha's later? She's having a few friends over to swim before her parents close the pool."

"Gosh, I'm surprised they still have it open." Mom glances at me. "Can you drop her on the way to work?"

This is the exact reason why I can't wait for Daisy to get her driver's license. "Sure."

Breakfast comes and goes, and I drop Daisy at Samantha's. *Few friends?* The place is packed with cars, and it's barely eleven in the morning.

"Don't tell Mom," Daisy says as she hops out.

I won't. I never do. Daisy's choices will catch up with her sooner or later.

Another few miles down the road and I pull into Patch and Paw Animal Hospital. I head straight for the boarders and Corn Chip, a beagle-schnauzer mix. He's here nearly every weekend. His mom travels a lot. Why have a pet if you're never around to love him, you know? I've always wanted a dog at home, but Mom doesn't like pets in the house. When I get my first place, I'm definitely getting a dog.

Corn Chip catches one look at me and does the whole-body-wiggle thing.

I love the little guy. He humanizes me. He is what makes me different from the profiles I obsess over. I have no urge to inflict pain on him or any other animal. Why would I? They're innocent. They only want love and a good rub. I do, however, have urges to inflict pain on those people who hurt animals. Big time.

I open the cage and let him out, along with a few others I know get along. As if I'm the pack leader, they follow me out the side door into the fenced yard.

I grab a few balls and give them a toss, and all four dogs take off, yipping and scrambling for the prized possession.

"Thought I'd find you out here."

Behind me stands Dr. Issa. At twenty-five he's the youngest veterinarian on staff. I've known him the two years I've worked here and met him back when he served as an intern.

Whereas my brother's smile tugs at my heart, Dr. Issa's shy, intelligent one massages the entire cardiac muscle. Tall, dark hair, brown eyes. Almost all the girls here have a crush on him that he never seems to notice.

Corn Chip runs over to him, and Dr. Issa gives him a total-body rub. "Doing surgery later. Want to assist?"

"Definitely." Dr. Issa always lets me assist in surgeries. I love watching the whole process. It's fascinating.

He smiles. "We'll scrub in at one."

"Okay."

"How'd your first few days at McLean High go?"

"Good."

Dr. Issa gives the ball a toss and all the dogs take off. "My brother's going there now. Maybe if you think of it, you can give him a hello?"

Welcoming new students is not really my thing, but this is Dr. Issa. "Is he a freshman?"

"No, junior. He used to go to a school in DC."

"Name?"

"Daniel Issa. I gave him your name too." He pauses. "I hope that's okay?"

This is so much more up Daisy's alley than mine, but again, this is Dr. Issa, so I give a little. "Sure. It's okay."

Later, during lunch, when I know everyone's either out of the building or in the break room, I grab the unused stolen tranquilizer from my Wrangler and head to the storage closet. I slip it back onto the shelf in line with the other vials.

The door opens and Dr. Issa steps in. "Oh, hi, didn't know you were in here." He glances to the tranquilizer section. "What are you doing?"

Putting stolen sedative back. Why do you ask? I grab the Acepromazine that I just put up, turn to him, and give a standard lie. "Doing a research project for school."

Dr. Issa takes it from my hand and puts it back on the shelf. "Careful. You really shouldn't be handling that without gloves."

I ignore how close he suddenly is to me and focus on the conversation. "Good for horses. Phenothiazine derivative. Causes profound lethargy followed by immobility. Potential for cardiac effects. If given intravenously will take effect within fifteen minutes."

Dr. Issa's dark brows lift. "I don't know why I'm constantly surprised by your intellect."

It doesn't take a genius to research on the Internet. And it doesn't take a genius to know I can't use Acepromazine now. After this conversation, the sedative is officially connected to me.

"So what questions do you have, then?" he prompts.

I want to ask him what he knows about etorphine but don't want that traced to me too. "None, I guess."

I'll wander back in here later and see if there's any on the shelves. However, since it's an elephant tranquilizer, I highly doubt there will be.

That'll be a black-market purchase.

Of course I have no clue how one goes about accessing the black market. I'm sure Reggie would know. Or could find out. The problem with that, though, entails letting Reggie into more of my life than I think either one of us is ready for. Reggie loves me like sisters should love each other, but sometimes I wonder if I reveal my true thoughts, I'll draw a line neither one of us is ready to cross.

Plus . . . I'm not entirely sure I want to kill my next victim. I'm glad I didn't kill the Weasel now. I'm glad I only made him suffer. Killing is so definitive. Years in jail leads to a more long-term type of justice.

But even though I'm not entirely sure I want to kill my next victim, I am entirely sure I *want* a next victim. Because the power it gives me, righting a wrong, the fright in the Weasel's eyes, the scared relief in the woman's . . . I think I've found my reason in this life.

Chapter Six

THE NEXT DAY IS SUNDAY, AND MOM GETS called in on an emergency I'm sure involves a serial killer.

"If I'm not going to be back by dinner, I'll call," she says, and rushes out.

I eye her soft leather carryall that she never locks. I've looked through it many times. I've read reports, studied pictures, copied notes on some of the more interesting cases. Mom has no clue I do it. I can't help it. Daisy likes to watch reality TV in her spare time, and I like to dig through Mom's briefcase. It's who I am.

"Will you put some of that horseradish mustard on it?" Justin asks, pulling me from my thoughts.

"Sure." I go back to his turkey-and-sprouts sandwich. I know, what eight-year-old likes turkey and sprouts, right?

He and I both have aikido class today—something our parents made all three of us take, but only he and I continue.

I like aikido because even though I'm skinny, I've learned to blend and redirect the motions of an attacker.

I can easily control and take down a two-hundred-pound opponent and have done so (in class) on many occasions. The Weasel was my first practice in the real world. Although he'd been short and pudgy, I'd say he was at least one hundred eighty pounds—a challenger for sure.

Daisy flings open the front door. "Zach, this is Lane and Justin."

In walks a guy I assume goes to our high school.

"Zach's new," Daisy announces. "He's a junior."

Zach nods. "Hi."

Daisy tugs him along. "We're going to my room."

Zach looks unsure about this as she pulls him up the stairs.

"That's not allowed," Justin reminds her.

"Whatever," she yells back.

"You going to tell Mom and Dad?" he asks me.

I shake my head.

"Mind if I do?"

"Knock yourself out, kid."

My sister's a slut. It's common knowledge she's already had sex several times, and according to gossip she gives okay hand jobs but is excellent at fellatio.

I walked in on her having sex last year. She didn't miss a beat as she kept riding the guy and glanced over to me in the doorway.

She'll end up pregnant. Watch. Or with an STD. Sometimes I wonder whatever happened to the little sister I carried two blocks home after she wrecked on her new bike. Of course I found out Terrence, the kid three streets over, made her wreck, and I went back and took care of him later, but I digress. Let's just say Terrence never messed with my sister again.

Zach comes back down the stairs and straight into the kitchen, surprising both me and my brother. "Saw the sandwiches. Mind if I make one?"

My brother and I exchange a glance.

I slide the fixings over and Zach helps himself.

"So," he begins, spreading mayo on one slice of wheat bread. "I've seen you around school. You're in the GT program?"

I nod.

He puts cheese on top of the mayo and then two slices of tomato. "You work at Patch and Paw, right?"

I take a bite of my sandwich. "Yes."

"Mike's my older brother."

"Dr. Issa?" Just saying his name flutters my insides a little.

Zach puts cucumber on top of the tomato, avoids the turkey and sprouts, and takes a huge bite. "Mm."

"He said your name is Daniel."

Zach shoots me a slightly surprised look. "He told you about me?"

"He wanted me to be your friend."

Zach laughs. "That sounds like Mike. Daniel's my first name. Mostly just my family calls me that."

My brother plucks a stray scrap of turkey from his plate and pops it into his mouth. "You a vegetarian?"

Zach nods.

Out of the corner of my eye I give him a solid look. Yes, I can now see the resemblance to Dr. Issa. Dark hair, dark, intelligent eyes, same boyish face.

Zach smiles, and I really see it then.

Daisy stomps down the stairs. "I thought you said you'd only be a second."

Zach lifts his sandwich. "Got hungry."

Justin laughs.

Daisy heaves a pouty sigh and heads back to her room.

I think I might like this Zach guy.

He turns to me. "My brother says you're really smart."

I've been in GT as long as I can remember. School comes easy for me. "I do okay."

Zach shoves another bite in. "Where you going to college?"

"UVA, hopefully."

"Medicine?" Zach whistles.

"Biology."

"Mike went to Hopkins."

"I know."

He finishes off his sandwich and tosses his napkin into the garbage. "Later. Nice to meet you both."

He lets himself out the front door, and Justin looks at me. "That was weird."

Yes it was. Most guys Daisy brings home disappear into her room and don't socialize with me and Justin. It's almost like Zach came over *to* socialize with me and Justin.

Daisy stomps back down. She's changed clothes to a skimpy tank and too-short mini. "Where's Zach?"

"He left!" Justin brightly informs her.

"He what?!" She turns on me. "What'd you say to him?"

"Nothing." *Why does she always assume I've done something?*

Daisy races out the front door. "Zach!"

"I like Zach," Justin tells me.

"Me too." His leaving will probably make Daisy want him even more.

I glance at the kitchen clock. "Let's get our *hakamas* on. I don't want to be late for aikido."

Fifteen minutes later we're heading out to the Wrangler, and Mom pulls in. "Heading to class?"

"You're back earlier than you thought," I observe.

She holds up her soft briefcase. "Brought the work home."

My brother rats out our sister. "Daisy had a boy in her room."

Mom sighs. "I'll handle it." She trudges toward the house, and I glance down at the briefcase, looking very puffy compared to when she left. Its lock is uncharacteristically pressed in. Luckily, I know where she keeps the key.

I'd rather skip aikido and rifle through her briefcase. And that's saying something because aikido has got to be about the best thing ever.

But I'll have to open the case tonight after everyone's gone to bed.

Chapter Seven

"WHAT ARE YOU DOING?" MY SISTER BUSTS ME
that night.

Nonchalantly, I shuffle the pictures I'd taken from Mom's
case under my notepad. "Last-minute homework."

"In Mom's office?"

I nod to her desktop. "She's got Excel."

Daisy narrows her eyes like she suspects I'm lying.

I ignore her and go back to the Excel file I had launched in
case this exact thing happened.

The thing about snooping around is that you have to do
it in the open to be most effective. If I had closed and locked
Mom's office, if I had scrambled to cover things up, or if I had
gotten real chatty, Daisy would be suspicious. Keeping things

out in the open allows me to fake honesty, fake normalcy.

My sister's the absolute last person I want having something on me.

"I got grounded," she tells me.

I nod. I know.

She sighs, and I hear more than see her scoot off. What the hell is she doing up at one in the morning anyway?

She gets something from the refrigerator, and then one of the stairs squeaks as she heads back up to her bedroom

I bring the pictures back out from under my notepad.

A female severed head stares back at me—brown eyes wide and blond hair matted to her head. Found in a swimming pool in Falls Church and identified as one Cynthia Hughes. Twenty-five years of age and a preschool teacher from a place just down the road.

The rest of the body is yet to be found.

According to the one and only report I've already read, the head was severed with a sharp knife. This case closely matches a decapitation that occurred this same time one year ago in Oregon, two years ago in Arizona, and three years ago in Tennessee.

"Closely matches" is the key phrase. There are some differences, but the report doesn't detail those.

I browse the document again—all the cases are unsolved and occurred exactly one year apart in the month of September. If it's the same killer, the FBI will find an arm next, then a leg, followed by the other arm and leg. The hands and feet get delivered at the very end in a cooler to the local police station.

I recognize this. Last year the Oregon decapitation made national news, and I added it to my journal. Looks like Mr. Decapitator Serial Killer has made his way to Northern Virginia and Washington, DC. My life can't get any better. A serial killer right in my own area. How great is that? Like I have a front-row seat to the latest feature.

I scan the picture of the head and the report and then send it to my e-mail. I put everything back exactly how I found it.

I glance around Mom's office. Her briefcase had been very full. So where's the rest of it? My gaze lands on her triple-locked file cabinet. Probably in there. I could pick it, but with three locks, it'd take a while.

The stair squeaks again, and my temper flares at my idiot sister. Why is she still up? I grab my stuff, head from the office, and run right into Mom.

She blinks. "What are you doing?"

It's not like my family to prowl the house this late. "I was using your computer to finish some homework."

"Oh." She yawns. "Well, get to bed. You've got school tomorrow." She heads into her office. "And I've got a case that's keeping me up." With that, she closes the door.

I just bet she's got a case that's keeping her up.

Mr. Decapitator, welcome to Washington, DC.

"I hope the man who did it gets life. . . ."

"No, didn't you hear? It was a woman. . . ."

"They say she got off. Something about an alibi . . ."

My ears perk up at this last part. The bell rings, and I head straight to the library for my TA job. Putting in for this gig was a calculated move. I knew it would give me a block of "me" time with the high-tech computer stations.

But being the good TA that I am, I go straight to the librarian first. "Mr. Bealles, anything you need me to do?"

He waves his hand as I know he will. "Nope. Do your homework."

I park it in front of a computer, log in, and immediately begin researching. This is something else Reggie taught me. To the common user, school computers are firewalled. But going in a back door permits unencumbered access to the Web. The kids that know this use it for Facebook or porn. I use it to research.

Yes, Lindsay got hit by a red Mini Cooper registered to a Heather Anderson. She claims her car was stolen and that she hadn't been driving. Her work associate corroborated her alibi, and she was released from police custody.

According to the report the driver of the stolen Mini ran from the crime scene and is still at large.

"Hi, Lane."

I glance over my shoulder to see Zach standing right behind me. He smiles. "Or should I say Slim?"

"Lane's fine."

He nods to my computer screen. "My gut tells me that woman's guilty."

My gut tells me the same thing.

"Someone needs to make her pay for what she's done."

Yes, someone does. But what an odd thing for Zach to say. I'm usually the only one to think those things. Or perhaps others have the thoughts but never put voice to them.

He comes around to stand beside me, and I get a hint of his boy-scented bodywash. "You going to the memorial service?"

I shake my head. Funerals are not for me. "You?"

"No." Zach leans his hip on the side of my computer desk. "I didn't even know her."

"True." I log out of the computer and stand, more to put space between us than anything. I don't care for people in my personal area. "See you later, then."

"Lane?"

I turn to see him still casually propped on the desk. "Yes?"

"Would you like to go out with me sometime?"

My freshman year I got asked out by a boy in the science club. My sophomore year it had been this guy that lives across the street. My junior year, science club again. I said no to all three of them. Dating just isn't something that interests me. Zach makes the fourth guy to ask me out, and I tell him what I told the other three. "No, thank you."

"Why not? Is it because I'm a junior?"

"No," I honestly tell him. "Aren't you dating Daisy or something?"

"No."

"Well, you should probably clarify that with her."

He nods. "Okay. Then will you go out with me?"

Persistent. I'll give him that much. "No."

"Hm." Zach pushes away from the desk. "Do you think I'm cute?"

I give him a good solid look. "Yes. You're not like most guys."

"How do you mean?"

"You're blunt and well-spoken."

"And most guys aren't?"

I think through all the boys I hear talking around school. "No, I don't consider a lot of them well-spoken."

Zach silently studies me. "I'll guess that you intimidate people."

"What about me is intimidating?"

"You're intelligent. Independent. And, clearly, you're not here to impress anyone."

I don't have a response. He's correct on all three accounts.

He takes a step toward me. "I'll see you around, Lane."

And with that he's gone.

If he asks me out again, I might say yes. Dating is, after all, what normal teenagers are supposed to do at night, right?

I don't exactly do normal things in the evenings. Plus, I'm a senior and I've never been on a date. Quite frankly, Dr. Issa is the only male to have elicited any type of female response in me. Dr. Issa's twenty-five, though. Eight years between us may not be a big deal when you're older, but it's a big deal now.

Yes, if Zach asks me out again, I'll probably say yes. He's cute, friendly, not an idiot, and it's the normal thing to do.

Chapter Nine

OVER THE NEXT WEEK I DO AS MUCH research as I can on the recently found severed head and suspected link to past killings. All I find are news articles, but I want the meat of the story. I want all the details reporters either don't have or brush over. It's in those details where I'll really get to know the serial killer, the Decapitator, as several reporters labeled him last year.

During this same week I do a little more research on the Heather Anderson drunk-driving case. In Northern Virginia, there are areas with red light cameras and areas without. Unfortunately, where Lindsay got hit and killed was in an area not covered by cameras. So Heather's stolen-car story cannot be corroborated one way or the other, hence the strength of the alibi.

Also during this same week I purposefully do not follow Heather. Not only does it heighten my own anticipation, it gives her time to get comfortable in her unindicted status. Because comfort leads to resuming normalcy, resuming normalcy leads to mistakes, and mistakes lead to her getting what she justly deserves.

On Tuesday night I follow her for the first time. She gets off work at six from a medical center where she's employed as a lab tech. Her Mini Cooper is still impounded, so in a rental car she stops by the grocery store and then heads home, where she stays for the rest of the night.

Same thing Wednesday and Thursday, and I begin to doubt my suspicions. Maybe her stolen-car story is true. On Friday she goes to happy hour with work friends. I park outside the restaurant/bar and write an entire ten-page essay for English class while I'm waiting for her to emerge.

At eleven p.m. she stumbles out arm in arm with her drunk work friends.

Here we go. I turn my dash-mounted camera on to record.

One of the coworkers climbs into a cab that's already waiting; the other lights up a cigarette and trips off down the sidewalk heading toward, I assume, the nearby apartment complex.

Heather fumbles with her key fob and finally gets behind the wheel. She swerves her way out of the parking lot and down the road. I crank my engine and slowly pull out. I knew I was right. I knew it.

Hovering in the right lane, she drives twenty miles *under* the speed limit, manages to brake at a yellow light, and runs a red light. I glance around, assure there are no cameras or cops, and gas my Jeep through the red light too.

She merges onto a highway, hangs in the right lane, swerving, overcorrecting, and gets honked at several times by passing cars. Then she exits, drives straight into and out of a shallow ditch, pulls in to a 7-Eleven convenience store, opens her door, and pukes. Gross.

She continues puking and I look away. Luckily, I'm not one of those people with a gag reflex. She wipes her mouth, and another mile down the road she turns in to a bar where some guy is waiting.

With a goofy, inebriated grin he staggers over and gets in.

They swing their way to a liquor store; Heather goes in and a few minutes later comes out with two black plastic bags heavy with bottles. I cannot believe the liquor store owner actually sold her more alcohol. He should be arrested just for that.

The two of them dive into the bags, crack open bottles, and continue drinking. It makes me sick just watching it. It's only been about a week since she ran Lindsay over, and she's so blasé about it. What, she has no conscience? She should have been scared straight into AA after what she did.

Across the street and down a couple of blocks sits a park.

Heather drives in the yellow turning lane the whole way, pulls straight into the park even though a sign says it's closed, crashes through a line of bushes, and comes to a stop on a soccer field. If this had been hours before, there'd still be families here. Heather would've plowed them right over. Just the thought of that disgusts me.

I watch as they both slowly pass out.

I hit the stop button and slip the tape out from the recorder. I'd like to go over and beat her up . . . or worse, but (a) she wouldn't feel it, and (b) this tape will do more long-term damage. Heather Anderson's officially busted, and while I'm not completely satisfied, while I'm not satiated, at least Lindsay and her family will get some justice for the tragedy in their lives.

I'm not satiated. . . . And I'm not sure when my next opportunity will come to be. With that thought lingering, I climb from my Jeep and stalk over to the car. I open the driver's door and stare down at Heather's pathetic, passed-out self. Lindsay had gone through the windshield. I'd say it's the least Heather deserves. But . . . I can't do that. It's taking things too far. I came for justice—not revenge.

The next morning I mail the tape unmarked to the cops with a *Sure she's innocent?* note inside. If the cops don't put her behind bars after this, I'll definitely hunt her down and make her pay. I *will* take things too far.

. . .

"Did you hear that woman who killed Lindsay is in jail?" I hear at school on Monday. "Someone trailed her and sent a video in."

"Maybe it was the Masked Savior," a guy jokes.

I really do hate that name.

Chapter Ten

THE NEXT NIGHT AT FAMILY DINNER VICTOR looks straight at Daisy. "*What* is wrong with you? You've been moping around this house for a week now." He looks at the rest of the family. "Hasn't she?"

They all nod, and so I nod too. Honestly, I haven't noticed, and truthfully, I really don't care.

My sister inhales through her nose and lets out a long, I'm-so-weary sigh. I don't know how Justin and I share her genetics. She's everything neither one of us has ever been.

"Know that guy Zach?" she begins.

My mom gives Victor a why-did-you-ask look.

He ignores her and turns to Daisy. "Yes, I've heard you talk about him."

Daisy picks at her chicken stir-fry. "He told me he just wants to be friends. And . . . I'm really upset because I think I may have loved him."

I've never been an eye roller, but if I were, this comment would deserve it.

"Friends are good," my mom diplomatically points out.

Daisy ignores her and looks straight at Victor. "I think he's emotionally damaged in some way. I think he's hiding something. I mean, he's new to our school, but I know his family's always lived here. So I asked him where he went to school before and he avoided the question. And then I heard he was in a mental institute."

"Daisy"—my mom gently reprimands her—"you know better than to listen to gossip."

"Well, why else wouldn't he like me?" Daisy snaps.

Where do I start?

"Maybe he likes someone else," my brother innocently suggests.

Daisy's bottom lip trembles, and I know this is about to turn into a drama fest.

"May I be excused?" I ask, already pushing back from the table and the chicken stir-fry I didn't finish. Victor does make a nice spicy one.

My mom nods as she checks her vibrating iPhone. "Need to take this," she tells the family, and disappears into her office.

I take my plate into the kitchen, my ears straining to make out her mumbling, muted voice. I bet anything it's about the recent severed head and suspected link to those past killings.

I wish I knew how to bug her office. And that thought sends me upstairs to my bedroom and my laptop. *Best way to bug a room*? I type into Google and begin browsing the hundreds of links.

Ugh. This is when Reggie comes in handy. She's like Google but precise. She can wade through the garbage and pinpoint what's needed. And so after only ten links I'm already frustrated and pick up my phone.

She answers after four rings. "Yo."

"I didn't think you'd pick up."

"Yeah, I'm eyeballs deep in Athlon versus Duron and the proof of which is . . ."

This is where I typically tune her out. Reggie speaks her own language. As usual I wait patiently, not listening, continuing to click through links.

"So what's up?" she finally asks.

"What's the best way to bug a room? I'm researching it right now and honestly just want to get to the point. You know how Google is."

"What room do you want to bug?"

"My room," I lie, knowing Reggie won't have a problem with that.

She laughs. "Why do you want to bug your room?"

I quickly make something up. "Because I think Daisy's snooping around, and I want to prove it."

"God, I'm glad I'm an only child."

Sometimes I wish I were, at least where my sister's concerned.

"Just do a nanny cam. Easy. Quick. You can buy one pretty much anywhere. They have audio, nonaudio. You can hide it on your bookshelf, in your alarm clock, in a stuffed animal. Yep, nanny cam."

Nanny cam. Hm. "Thanks, Reg."

"No, prob."

I only hope it's as easy and quick as Reggie says.

Chapter Eleven

THE VERY NEXT DAY I PURCHASE A NANNY cam hidden in a clock. I choose a popular model that is carried by several major electronics retailers. I pay cash for it, and no one blinks an eye.

At home I put the nanny-cam clock in Mom's office. Every evening I'll plan on swapping out the memory card, browsing the recordings on my laptop, and using whatever I can to build my personal file on the Decapitator. I want to know everything I can about his disgusting, warped mind. Some would call it a sick fascination. But it's my fascination.

I want to know who he is. How he picks his victims. But most importantly, why he does what he does. How long he's been doing it. What his methods are. What his childhood was like. In fact, I can't think of anything better than sitting down and having a conversation with a person like that. Just an hour to probe his brain. Discover what made him who he is. See if there are any parallels to my own darkness.

And then I'd remind him about all the innocents he'd harmed. I'd detail their murders for him. I'd make him relive his sins right before I'd make him suffer the same way he made them. It would be the most perfect retribution of all time. But someone of the Decapitator's caliber is out of my reach right now. He's something I'll one day work up to.

And how I'll look forward to that day.

"You okay?"

I snap out of my fantasizing and over to my mom. "Yes." I slide her the to-go mug I've already made. "I accidentally broke your office clock. I got you a new one and set it up. Sorry about that."

"Oh, heavens, Lane, that's fine. You didn't have to get me a new one."

"I wanted to." And bugging her office goes that easy.

"Did some woman's arm get thrown off a bridge?" Justin pipes up.

Mom chokes on her coffee. "Where did you hear that?"

I tune in. Yes, where did he hear that?

Justin points to the muted morning news where two reporters sit talking. In the upper-right-hand corner of the screen is a tiny picture of the 495 overpass with an animated arm flying off of it.

My mom snatches the remote and turns the TV off.

I bet that was her mystery phone call from the other night. Someone on her team calling to report the arm.

She grabs her iPhone and speed-dials a number. "Who the *hell* released . . . ," she begins, and then slams her office door.

Mom rarely gets upset. This must be a *huge* deal.

At school during my TA job, Reggie texts me. CAN U TALK?

I immediately dial her number. "You okay?"

"I had sex."

"Um . . . okay." This is surprising. She's worse than me when it comes to all that social stuff.

"I didn't know you were seeing someone."

"I'm not. It was the guy across the hall in my dorm."

This is why they shouldn't allow coed dorms, I want to say, but of course I don't. "Everything okay?"

"Yeah. It was . . . eh. I'm glad it's over with. I just wanted somebody to tell, and you're always the first person I think of."

That comment softens my heart. "I hear it gets better after the first time."

"Maybe." She laughs, but it doesn't have any humor to it. "Guess it's your turn now."

I hate how sad she sounds. "I'm in no hurry."

"I wasn't either, but I'm nineteen and feeling a bit behind schedule."

"Reggie, that's ridiculous."

"I know, which makes me even madder. I'm too smart to have those thoughts."

"Well, don't do it again unless you want to. Promise?"

She doesn't answer at first. Then, "Yeah, promise."

Although Reggie's never admitted it, I think she secretly wishes she had been born less brilliant. That she had been this normal teen that maybe played sports or did cheer or something instead of having a dazzling mind that tested out of high school at fourteen.

"Anyway, all good with the nanny cam?" She changes subjects.

"All good." I refocus on the computer screen in front of me with the Decapitator arm story. "Hey, Reg? Can you dig some info up on the Decapitator? He's a serial killer, and he's actually in our area right now. Mom's working the case."

"You do know your fascination with killers is creepy, right?"

I know she's joking, but it still tweaks a nerve. "Never mind."

"No! Of course I'll dig some stuff up."

"My mom's just as fascinated," I defend myself. "She does it for a living."

"I know. It's okay. I'm sorry."

Neither one of us says anything for a few seconds, and I sign off first. "Bell's about to ring. Catch you later."

"Lane—"

I hang up on her. I know she's sorry she said it. But all day long her comment is all I can think about. *Creepy.* It's the same word Daisy used. Reggie's always been the one person I've been most honest with. The one person I've been most myself with. Maybe we're at the point in our friendship where that can't be anymore. Maybe we're at the stage where we start becoming more ourselves and less dependent on each other's emotional support.

Maybe . . . but hopefully not. I can't imagine not having Reggie. The truth is I probably won't have Reggie anymore if she finds out my true self.

After school I drop my brother and sister back home and head straight to the Patch and Paw clinic.

"What are you doing here?" Dr. Issa asks. "You're not on the schedule."

"Is Corn Chip around?"

Dr. Issa smiles, and my cardiac muscle experiences that massage. It's interesting; most days my heart simply fills a voided chest cavity. Logically I know it's in there, but when he smiles I *know* it's in there. It's very simple, this attraction I have for him—he's a vet, he's smart, he's nice to me, and he's hot. Also, we click in this interesting way I've never really experienced before. Like there's this magnetism between us that carries the possibility for a powerful explosion.

"Yes," Dr. Issa says. "He's in his usual space."

When I walk into the boarding facility, Corn Chip's gray eyebrows come down over his dark eyes like he's pissed I've let so many days go by since our last visit.

"I'm sorry, C-squared," I apologize as I unlock his cage.

He tries to act indifferent but within seconds gives in to the excitement of seeing me.

This is why I prefer dogs to humans. You're good to them; they're good to you. You're shitty to them, and they'll get you back sooner or later. Most important, they don't hold a grudge.

I lead Corn Chip into the side yard and toss the ball with him a couple times. I think he can tell I'm just not into it today. He sniffs around my feet and then sits and focuses his dark eyes up at me.

I squat down and give him a rub on the tips of his ears where I know he likes it the most. Closing his eyes in bliss, he leans in to me. I inhale his wonderful scent: dryer sheets mixed with a big bag of corn chips. His mom picked a great name for him, that's for sure.

I don't normally talk to dogs. For that matter I don't normally talk to humans.

But Corn Chip's unconditional love and the fact we're alone in the yard causes me to say, "I don't know what to do with myself." *Even Reggie thinks I'm creepy.*

Corn Chip stops leaning in to me and looks up like he's surprised I spoke.

I know it's not normal that I'd rather be researching the Decapitator than going out on a date. Should I force myself into a more typical mold just to blend in?

"Should I get sex over with like Reggie did?"

The tip of Corn Chip's scraggly tail vibrates.

I mean, I've always understood it in terms of procreation, but other than that, I really don't care. Frankly, it's too messy an act. I'd rather keep my bodily fluids to myself.

Corn Chip looks beyond me. I stand and turn to see Dr. Issa behind me. *Should I get sex over with like Reggie did?*

Oh no. He heard me say that.

He starts to move back—"Sorry"—and I step right up and kiss him.

Dr. Issa immediately breaks contact. "Uh-uh—"

I turn away from his red face and whistle for Corn Chip. I can't believe I just kissed Dr. Issa. What is wrong with me? I don't do things like that.

I tune in to myself and realize I'm actually embarrassed. I can't remember the last time that happened. Embarrassment isn't an emotion that normally occurs for me.

As quickly as I can, I tuck Corn Chip into his cage and hightail it out to my Jeep. I crank the engine, and as I pull away, I touch my fingers to my lips.

Did I really just kiss Dr. Issa?

Chapter Twelve

IN MY ROOM LATE THAT NIGHT I PULL UP the nanny-cam footage, programmed to only record when there's movement in the office.

I see my mom looking at several pictures of the decapitated head and several more of the actual arm, not the one they showed on the news.

I freeze-frame the arm pictures and zoom in. Like the head, the same neatly cut skin marks the shoulder where a knife sliced it. I don't imagine it's a regular old butcher knife. Clean skin like that would take a sword of some sort.

Mom looks at a report next, but I can't make out the details. I'll see if it's in her briefcase later. I pull up Word and type in some questions:

1. How is the Decapitator preserving the parts?
2. How was the arm thrown off the bridge? By a pedestrian? From a vehicle?
3. How was the victim picked?
4. What is the significance about the month of September being the kill month?
5. Who is leaking all this to the media?
6. Why a whole year in between kills?

Someone knocks on my door, and I minimize my screen. "Come in."

My mom peeks her head in. "This came for you." She tosses me a tiny, flat envelope.

"Thanks."

"You doing okay, Lane?"

"Sure. Why?" *Have I been acting weird?*

She smiles. "No reason. You're always so quiet, stoic. I feel like I take your happiness for granted." She laughs. "Your sister wears her emotions on her sleeve and you do everything but. I have to do my mom job and check in with you."

"I'm good. Really."

She studies me for a long, thoughtful second. "You're so much like your father. I wish you could've known him."

"Me too," I agree, feeling the sadness I always get when she brings him up. He died before I was born, but Mom's always had nothing but good things to say about him. He'd been a decorated marine who died tragically while kayaking. His father, my grandfather, had been a pastor. His mother, my grandmother, a stay-at-home mom. They both passed before he'd even turned twenty, and when my father died, it had ended that family line. Well, except for me.

My mom chuckles a little, like her thoughts had wandered off too, into another time. "Well, anyway, I love you, Lane."

"I love you, too."

She nods to the envelope. "Who's that from?"

I give it a quick glance. "Reggie." Although I doubt it is. But Reggie has been and always will be a justifiable, parent-friendly name that requires no additional response.

Mom smiles. "Good night, then."

She leaves, and I look at the envelope, type-addressed to me with no return address. I tear it open and pull out a white card.

On it is glued a picture of the decapitated head, a picture of the severed arm, and a new one of a leg. Across the bottom is typed:

THIS IS A PRESENT.
TELL ANYONE AND I *WILL* HURT YOU.

I swallow as I read the typed words again. This is from the Decapitator. Oh my God. He knows me. He knows where I live. He probably knows I've been researching him.

My hand shakes as I take in the pictures of the body parts and the words again. If he knows where I live, he knows I have a family. He's got to know my mom is the FBI lead.

This is a present. Why would he be sending me a present?

A very tiny arrow in the bottom right corner catches my attention then and has me flipping the card over. On the back is a small picture of me coming out of school and below that is typed:

I KNOW EVERYTHING ABOUT YOU.

My shaking hand transforms to a full-on wobble, and I put the picture down. I close my eyes and sit for second, trying to regain equilibrium. I inhale a deep breath and blow it out slow. My heart thumps an unusually deep rhythm, and it distracts me for a few seconds. I tune in to it and realize I'm definitely scared, but I'm also excited. Yes, thrilled, in fact, to have been contacted personally by a real-life serial killer.

Tell anyone and I will hurt you. I believe him. Of course I believe him. Hurt *me* personally, hurt me by going after my family, or both? He's certainly capable of it all.

I've researched nearly every killer out there, and there's a reason for everything they do. There's a reason he's contacted me. Perhaps to kill me, but my instincts say no. It's more likely he wants my mom. He's picked the wrong disturbed daughter if that's his plan.

I open my eyes, more calm now, and pick the picture back up. As far as I know, he hasn't publicly revealed the leg yet.

All are shrink-wrapped, which answers my previous preservation question. I bring the paper closer to my eyes and study it. Grotesque. I'm repulsed, but I'm also drawn in. Mesmerized. Curious of the facts and details just like I'd been with the Weasel.

As I study the picture, my mind narrows to three main questions:

Why send this to me?

How does the killer know I've been researching him?

And what does he want me to do with this?

Chapter Thirteen

ZACH COMES UP BESIDE ME THE NEXT DAY
as I'm spinning the combination on my locker. "Hey, you."

I haven't spoken to him since the library when he asked me
out. "Heard you were in a mental institution." I always like to
get right to the point.

Zach laughs. "This is why I like you, Lane. There's no pre-
tense with you."

I grab my science folder. So he's emotionally damaged. Join
the club.

"Yes, I spent some time in rehab," he admits.

"Alcohol? Drugs?"

"Alcohol. Haven't touched any in twelve months and seventeen days."

I close my locker. "What made you drink?"

"God, I think I just fell a little harder for you."

I don't know why. All I did is ask him a question.

"Our mom died. Mike never told you?"

"Why would Dr. Issa tell me that?"

"I got the impression you two are close."

"We work together, that's all." I think of the kiss and what his smile does to me and wonder if he'd ask me out if I were older.

"Anyway, when I got out of rehab, Dad gave me a choice of going back to private school or coming here, and I chose here."

The warning bell rings and I start off down the hall.

Zach follows. "I cleared things up with your sister."

"I know."

"Let me guess. Drama?"

Zach has no idea.

"So go out with me?"

I sidestep someone in the hall as I mull that question over. I *had* told myself if he asked me out again, I'd say yes. It's the regular teenage thing to do. "Okay. Where?"

It takes him a second to realize I just said yes. "Hockey? Sunday afternoon game?"

I round the hall toward the GT wing. "I'll meet you there."

"Great. I'll give you the details later."

As I head into my class, I glance back, but he's already gone.

I don't know why I glance back. It's not like I expect him to be standing there staring after me.

All day long I physically go through the routine of school, but every class I'm in I stare out the window wondering if the Decapitator's staring back. I spend my whole day thinking about his communication. Maybe he somehow knows I'm the Masked Savior. Maybe he saw me.

Or perhaps he's like Reggie, has his cyberfingers in everything, and knows I've been researching him. Maybe he traced an IP address or something.

More important, what does he want me to do with the knowledge that he knows me now? Does he want me to keep researching him, or maybe he wants to play some weird game of hide-and-seek? Just the thought of that not only frightens me, but also entrances me. The things I can learn if I play along . . .

Later after school, Daisy's already out in the parking lot waiting at the Wrangler. "You're a bitch."

I climb in the Jeep. So what's new?

"Samantha overheard Rachel say that she saw you talking in the hall with Zach."

What, I can't talk to Zach?

"Samantha overheard Rachel say that Zach asked you out."

This is why high school annoys me. This is why people annoy me.

Daisy tears up. "I can't believe *you're* the other girl!"

"Oh, would you get over yourself?" I snap.

Daisy's eyes go wide.

"Yes, Zach and I were talking. Yes, we're going out on Sunday. Daisy, you need to grow up. You think you can whine and pout and flirt your way out of every issue. It might work with some people. It sure as hell doesn't work with me, and clearly it doesn't work with Zach. Move on with your life. Jesus!"

Daisy doesn't speak. I don't blame her. I've never raised my voice to anyone. Thinking about the Decapitator all day long has put me a bit on edge. Yes, I've never raised my voice, but I can't think of a person who deserves it more than my sister.

I park in the elementary school's kiss-and-ride, and Justin runs out. Daisy silently moves into the backseat, and Justin climbs in the front.

He hands me a flyer. "Do you think Mom can give me stuff to donate?"

I glance through the flyer detailing a family's house that burned down. The school's organized a fundraiser to replace what was lost.

Justin buckles his seat belt. "One of the kids is in my grade, one's in kindergarten, and another one's still a baby. They lost everything."

I hand him back the flyer. "Mom won't have a problem. I'll help you when we get home."

"How'd the fire start?" Daisy finally speaks.

"Arkenic?" He shakes his head. "Ar . . . ar . . ."

"Arson?" I provide.

He points at me. "That's it!"

How sad they lost everything. I can't imagine. "Do they know who?"

Justin shakes his head.

Someone needs to pay for making that family suffer. The edginess that had been simmering in me all day heats to a slight boil. The familiar itch raises its scratchy little head. Arson. Maybe I can find out who. Trail the guy. Scratch my itch. Cool the boil. Yes, this is exactly what I need right now.

Daisy doesn't speak to me the whole rest of the afternoon and evening, and believe me, it's a welcome relief.

After dinner the whole family scours the house for items to donate to the family in need.

By ten p.m. I'm in my room. I pull up the nanny-cam footage from last night and listen to Mom's conversation.

". . . I agree with Bill," Mom's saying. "The media leak is on the outside. I feel strongly it's not an inside source."

She stops and listens to the other end of the conversation. "Profilers say it's the Decapitator leaking the information?" She huffs a laugh. "This guy's got a high opinion of himself."

The person on the other end talks for a while. Mom responds, "Reports indicate the arm was thrown from a vehicle moving approximately ten miles per hour." She listens for a few seconds. "Yes, I agree. I think the person was riding a bike."

A serial killer who rides a bike, leaks information to the media, and who has contacted me directly. He's interesting. This is for sure.

I want to text Reggie, but after the "creepy" comment I'm hesitant. Reggie and I don't say things like that to each other. We've always accepted one another for our odd selves. It's an integral part of our friendship. It's the one thing I value the most.

Back to nanny cam, I save the file and do the only thing I can at this point: dig into researching the recent arson. Taking this guy down will relieve the tension in me. It'll help me regain my equilibrium.

When I find the arsonist, I think I'll deal with him by setting him on fire. Or maybe I'll just burn down where he lives too. I'll have to think on it for sure.

I bring up the news feed on my laptop and read the paragraphs. Five days ago at approximately four in the morning an unknown person poured gasoline around the perimeter of a twelve-hundred-square-foot home. The mother and baby were asleep in the master bedroom with the two older children in a separate room. The father was gone on a business trip. Currently there are no suspects.

I'll lay odds it's the dad. He came home from his trip a day early. Set the house on fire. Planned on collecting not only home insurance but also life insurance on his family.

Yes, I'll bet anything it's the dad. And starting tomorrow I have someone new to trail. Electricity zings through my synapses, stimulating me for the pursuit. An arsonist. Someone new to add to my now-growing repertoire. The question is, what will I do to him when I catch him?

Chapter Fourteen

THE ARSON FAMILY IS STAYING AT AN extended-stay hotel. I spend two nights in the hotel parking lot with my binoculars, watching the dad come home, the kids exuberantly greeting him, and he genuinely exhibiting happiness toward them. I observe as he helps with homework and bath time and plays with each kid.

I've got a good stepdad, but this guy can easily win the father of the year award, he's that perfect.

Except . . . he and the wife rarely interact. And that—my gut tells me—is the key.

On Friday night I watch him pack for yet another business trip. He takes a taxi to the airport, and the mom sits in the hotel living room for hours, watching TV while the third grader makes sandwiches. The child gives one of those sandwiches to the mom, dresses the younger one for bed, gives the baby a bottle, and when the baby cries, picks her up and soothes her.

Clearly, he's used to this routine. And all the while the mom sits zoned out in front of the TV. I'm not entirely sure she's even watching it.

At eleven thirty the kids are all asleep in one bed, the mom has passed out in the living room, and I need to go home. Not only do I have a curfew, but I have to work the early shift at Patch and Paw. Plus . . . I want to see Dr. Issa. I want to see how he reacts to me after the kiss I unexpectedly gave him.

Tomorrow rolls around, but by one p.m. Dr. Issa still hasn't shown up at work, which isn't that odd. In the two years I've worked here, he has missed several days.

"Where's Dr. Issa?" I ask the receptionist.

She shrugs. "Called in sick."

Sick because he's really sick or sick because I kissed him?

WE STILL ON FOR SUN? Zach texts me.

Okay, that annoys me. If I've made plans, then I'll be there. Why do people always insist on the need to double-check everything?

YES, I type back.

DID U GET MY NOTE? TIME & PLACE?

YES, I respond. If I hadn't, I would've already followed up. Don't mean to be a bitch here, but common sense.

Thankfully, he doesn't text me back with a smiley face or other cute lingo.

At the end of my shift I leave work, text my mom with HEADING TO LIBRARY, and then go straight to the extended-stay hotel. I park and get out my binoculars, and it's like a day hasn't even passed.

The mom's still sitting in the same spot, wearing the same sweatpants and oversize T-shirt, staring at the TV that's now not even on.

The kids are out on the tiny balcony, playing.

Hours go by and night settles in. I'm not sure when the dad is coming back, but I hope it's soon.

I've heard of postpartum depression. Is this it?

Abruptly the mom stands up, and I nearly jerk to attention. She yells for the kids, and they excitedly go running. She grabs her purse and ushers them all out into the parking lot and into a Montero.

The oldest buckles the baby into a safety seat, checks on the other's seat belt, and then fastens his own. The SUV pulls from the lot, and I follow a safe distance behind as they visit a Burger King drive-through.

Normally kids are cheery, babbling, singing on family outings, especially ones involving fast food. It strikes me how all three kids are exceptionally still.

She drives to a Target next, parks the SUV, says something to the kids, gets out, closes the door, and walks off. She keeps on walking, right past Target, right past a string of restaurants, hangs a left on a side road, and disappears from sight.

I stay in my Wrangler a few aisles over, watching the Montero, waiting, waiting, waiting for I don't know what—the mom to come back—*something* to happen.

I want to go to the kids. I want to tell them it's going to be okay. I want to drive off and find the mom. I want to call someone but don't want my cell traced.

As inconspicuously as possible I glance around at all the security cameras. Target is not my ideal place. I glance at my watch. At this point I've been sitting here thirty-two minutes. Anybody reviewing this footage will wonder why I haven't gotten out.

And they'll probably wonder why I'm here at nine thirty at night.

Fortunately for me Target is still hopping on a Saturday evening, so me and my Wrangler don't stick out too much.

The door to the Montero suddenly opens and out crawls the third grader. He unbuckles his baby sister from the car seat, props her on his hip, grabs the hand of the kindergartner, and starts right toward me.

I sit as still as possible, watching them silently, expressionlessly cross the Target parking lot.

If their mom was here right now, I'd taser her just for putting them through this.

It becomes so clear to me. *She* set that house on fire. *She* wanted these beautiful kids dead. *She* gave up on them. And she better be glad she walked away. I would've killed her if I'd caught her trying to hurt them again.

The three children draw closer, and I roll my window down in expectation. There's no way I can avoid getting involved.

"Hi, babies, where are your parents?"

I look to the right, where an elderly lady is pushing a cart with a toddler in the seat.

The third grader breaks eye contact with me and turns to the elderly lady. "I think our mom left us," he bravely tells her.

I roll my window up and hang out a bit while the lady calls for help, police eventually show up, and the three children are taken into custody.

As I pull from the parking lot, I catch sight of Dr. Issa's silver Nissan Juke. I do a double take and see the Hopkins sticker on the back that verifies it's his. That's odd. I wonder how long he's been here and . . . if he saw me.

I briefly consider waiting, just to see, but then decide that's not a good idea. I need to get out of here. I drive from the parking lot and head in the direction the mom walked. I drive around for a while, looking, not expecting to find her, but I don't know, maybe hoping I'll see her.

Hopefully, by tomorrow the kids will be reunited with their father. And by tomorrow there's no telling where the mom will be.

A thought slams into me then, and I nearly brake to a stop. Has the Decapitator been watching me tonight as I watched them?

Chapter Fifteen

"WHAT ARE YOU UP TO TODAY?" VICTOR asks me over Sunday breakfast.

"Catching a hockey game with Zach," I answer, not even glancing at Daisy.

"Zach?" Mom looks between me and my sister.

"I like Zach," Justin chimes in.

Daisy shoves a huge bite of pancake into her mouth.

"Thought I'd go to the driving range." Victor wisely changes the subject. "Justin, you in?"

"Sure!"

Mom motions to the corner where two huge Target bags sit. "I bought some things for that family at Justin's school. Lane, mind dropping them on your way to hockey?"

My mom really is the greatest. "When'd you go to Target?"

"Last night. Why?"

Because I was there too, rescuing children from a runaway mother. "No reason. I swung in too, that's all." That statement will explain my presence in case parking-lot footage makes the news.

"I saw that cute doctor from your clinic. Dr. Issa?"

I perk up. "In Target?"

"Yeah, he was buying all kinds of stuff. Looked like he had quite a home improvement project going on."

He never mentioned a home improvement project to me. Then again, why would he? "Did he see you?"

"No, don't think so." Mom reaches for the orange juice, and that ends our discussion on Dr. Issa and Target.

A few hours later I load the bags into the Wrangler and head to Justin's school, where a drop box has been set up outside for donations.

I swing by the extended-stay hotel next and see the Montero parked in the lot. Through the hotel window I catch the dad feeding the baby and talking on the phone. There's an older gentleman reading to the two other kids, and I assume he must be the grandfather.

The mom is nowhere to be seen. I hope I can find her. She deserves punishment for what she did. And those kids and the father deserve vengeance. I'll give it one more day and google her name and see what's been reported.

Those poor kids. At least they've got a great dad.

From the extended stay it's off to DC and hockey. I meet Zach outside the Verizon Center.

He smiles at me. "Hey, you."

I like the way he greets me. It's cute. I smile back—"Hi"—and suddenly realize I am genuinely pleased to be here with him.

He leads the way in. "Ever been to hockey?"

"I have. A few times."

Zach gives the attendant our tickets and leads me straight to a hot dog stand. "I assume you eat hot dogs?"

I eat everything. "Mustard only."

He orders a veggie dog for himself and a couple of Cokes and directs me to our seats.

One bite in I ask, "Didn't see Dr. Issa at work yesterday. Everything okay?"

Zach nods but doesn't elaborate. I've never been one to press an issue, so I table the subject.

I lick mustard off my thumb, glad it's not spicy. I'm a French's-plain girl all the way. "What's up with the vegetarian thing?"

He wipes his mouth. "Mom and Dad raised Mike and I meatless. That's all. No animal-rights drama."

I think about all the times I've seen Dr. Issa eating lunch. "Your brother eats meat."

Zach laughs. "Who are you, the meat police?"

He's right. It's none of my business.

"Kidding, Lane. Yes, Mike eats meat. Just because they raised us vegetarian doesn't mean we can't choose for ourselves."

I guess I can't imagine *not* eating meat. I am a carnivore, through and through.

We watch the game, eat our dogs, and drink our Cokes while everyone around us yells and cheers.

I search my brain for something to say and come up with absolutely nothing. Talking has never been my strong suit, and frankly I thought Zach would have a lot to say. I thought he'd carry the conversation. I thought I could just nod, insert a comment here or there, make an acknowledging grunt, and the whole date would be done before either of us realized it.

It's not like I'm having a bad time. I like hockey. I like hot dogs. I like mustard. And the more I sit here beside Zach, the more I like his scent—a nice mixture of laundry detergent and that same bodywash I caught on him in the library.

I tune in to him then. *Really* tune in to him. To his dark hair and his snug T-shirt. To the curve of his biceps, his flat stomach, and the fit of his faded jeans. He's taller than me—I'd guess over six feet—and sports the body of a baseball player.

I take my gaze away from his strong thigh and look straight up into his face to find his brown eyes focused on me.

He trails those eyes down to my lips.

The lights go out as period intermission begins. Only a

spotlight illuminates the rink, where a girl is ice-skating to a rocking beat.

Zach is still staring at my lips.

I lick them, and he takes that as his cue to immediately lean in.

There is no softness, no teasing. There's only tongues and hunger. Fortunately, I like it. Unfortunately, I'm thinking of Dr. Issa.

The lights come on and we pull away from each other. Zach is breathing heavily. I focus on myself and note I'm not. I want to be, though.

The Zamboni enters and begins resurfacing the ice in prep for the second period.

Zach smiles at me at the exact second a scream pierces the air. Then another scream. And then another.

Zach and I look around, trying to figure out what's going on, and there it is, hanging half in/half out of the Zamboni—a severed leg.

To my surprise Zach doesn't even react. "Would you look at that?" is all he says.

Yes, would you look at that. But more importantly—I glance around the crowd—is the Decapitator looking at it too?

Chapter Sixteen

THE WHOLE STADIUM IS SHUT DOWN, everyone with access to the ice is questioned, security film is reviewed, and the FBI is called in.

The footless leg does indeed belong to the previous discovered head and arm. If things go according to plan, the killer will reveal the other arm and leg next.

My question, though—does he plan to include me in the next revelation? Or maybe he'll send me another card.

I'm sure he knew I was going to be at the hockey game and he left the leg for me. His bizarre way of letting me know he's tracking me.

I zero in on myself and try to analyze how this affects me. . . . I'm excited to have seen a severed leg in person, albeit from a distance. Eager to perhaps receive another letter from him. Thrilled that he's including me. And yes, scared. *Tell anyone and I will hurt you.*

Which brings me back to why me. Also pondering the fact I'm both anticipatory and frightened that a serial killer is personally contacting me.

The entire thing incessantly circles my brain as I make French-press coffee Monday morning. I love the early mornings when I'm the only one up. Five a.m. is my natural alarm clock, which gives me at least an hour of "me" time before normal people get up.

I take my cup of dark brew over to the dining room table and log on to my laptop. As I'm waiting for it to come up, I check my phone for messages.

I have three.

From Zach: SEE U AT SCHOOL. The time stamp shows it was sent fifteen minutes ago. Looks like somebody else is an early riser too.

From Reggie: REQUESTED INFO IN YOUR INBOX. SORRY I CALLED U CREEPY.

THAT'S OK, I type back. I AM CREEPY. She'll get a kick out of that.

I pull up my inbox to see half a dozen files attached. Quickly I browse them. Sure enough, she's hacked her way into whatever necessary system to get me information on the Decapitator.

As I look through them, it hits me like a kick to the gut. If he's tracing my research through IPs, then he'll know Reggie's supplied this. I'm an idiot. I involved Reggie before I even realized the Decapitator was tracking me. I immediately pick up the phone and call her even though I know she's not up yet. It goes straight to voice mail.

"Reg, don't send me anything else on the Decapitator. And do whatever you need to do to cover your cybertracks. I got in trouble with Mom," I lie. There's no way I'm going to tell her the Decapitator contacted me directly.

I hang up and go back to the third text message. It's from a number I don't recognize. DID U LIKE THE GIFT? Attached is a picture of the severed footless leg hanging out of the Zamboni. My heartbeat kicks into hyperdrive. He knows my number. Of course he knows my number. This shouldn't surprise me.

Quickly, I forward the message and picture to my inbox and bring it up full screen on my laptop.

Like the head and the arm, it has obviously been removed with a sharp object. And like the head and the arm, it was shrink-wrapped for preservation.

At least this answers my question. The Decapitator knew I was going to be there. He left the stump as a present for me.

Victor comes downstairs, surprising me. "You're up early," I observe.

He puts an overnight bag by the front door. "Got a flight to catch. You sleep okay?"

"Always." Sleep rarely eludes me. I don't toss or turn. I typically wake in the exact position I fall asleep in. I read somewhere that's the sign of a good conscience.

And I seldom if ever dream. Or maybe I do dream and just don't remember it.

Victor grabs a banana from the kitchen, kisses the top of my head, and glances at my computer screen. "Lane, what are you looking at?"

I play it cool. "This is the leg that came out of the Zamboni at yesterday's hockey game."

"I know that. But where did you get that picture? And more important, why are you looking at it?"

"The picture's all over. There were hundreds of people at the game." I zoom in a little closer. "I know Mom's on the case. I'm interested I guess."

"Mom said she's going to talk to you today about it. See if you're okay. Were you scared?"

"Honestly, I barely even saw what happened. It was all so quick."

He studies me for a second. "Okay. But if you feel like discussing it, you know your mom and I are here for you."

"I know. Thanks."

He nods to the screen. "Please don't be looking at that when your brother comes down."

"I won't."

He gives my shoulder a squeeze and is out the door. I wonder what he and mom would do if they found out the Decapitator is contacting me. They would freak. They would put our whole family in protective custody. They would in turn put me at risk. Put themselves at risk. A move like that would piss the Decapitator off. He wouldn't back away. Protective custody or not, he'd find me. He's evaded being caught for years. He's good. There's no doubt in my mind he couldn't find me if he really wanted.

He's chosen me for a reason.

I study his text for a second, deciding. . . . I select call and hold my breath for what might happen. It rings exactly one time then clicks over to "This call cannot be completed as dialed." I release my breath. It's probably a throwaway cell.

I catalog the text message and picture with my other files, password-protect them, and transfer them to my flash drive. Then I google the arson case.

The mother's body was found floating in someone's swimming pool. According to the police report she drowned herself. This is disappointing news. Not that she's dead, but that I wasn't involved. My internal itch raises its inflamed, scratchy head. I'll have to find someone else to relieve it.

Those poor kids. Now they have to deal not only with their mom leaving them but also with her committing suicide.

And the dad. Left all alone to care for three young children. He had to have seen it coming. The mom seemed so out of it.

It occurs to me then: The Decapitator took the life of someone who wanted to live, and yet here is this mother who wanted to die.

It's too bad the Decapitator and the mother couldn't have gotten together. They could've solved each other's problems.

Which brings me back around to my questions. How does the Decapitator pick his victims? And why the month of September?

The shower goes on upstairs. My family's getting up. I use the few extra minutes to pull up Reggie's information again. In addition to Oregon, Arizona, and Tennessee, the Decapitator did three others, two years apart instead of one. Add Minnesota, Maine, and Wyoming to the list. I glance through all the victims' names and don't immediately see any similarities.

I need to figure out the parallel points and why he changed from two years apart to one. Also—I zoom in on an old picture—he used a dull knife and then switched to a sharp one. There's got to be a connection between it all. A connection well hidden, otherwise the FBI would've already figured it out. Or perhaps they *have* figured it out and have chosen not to release information to the public. A killer doesn't just randomly pick victims and methods.

Unless . . . the Decapitator has been fine-tuning his technique. Like I am with my kit. It's a learning process as you go along.

Our front door opens and Ercita walks in. I'd forgotten she was coming today. I glance at my laptop clock. Six fifteen a.m. As usual, she's right on time.

Ercita's our housekeeper. She only comes once a month and spends the whole day sanitizing our home from the ceiling fans on the second floor down to the lumpy couch in our basement.

She's approved through the FBI, which is why my mom hired her some five years ago.

"Good morning, Lane." She closes the door and goes straight into the laundry room.

Something's wrong. Ercita never walks past me without sitting and talking.

She comes out of the laundry room and goes into the bathroom. Seconds later she crosses right in front of me and into the living room to turn on the TV.

"Ercita, what's wrong?"

She turns and—oh my God—there's tears in her eyes. I'm not good with tears.

"Federico didn't show up."

I know she's been saving money to bring her brother from El Salvador to America. Just like she brought her sister and their mother. "What do you mean didn't show up?"

She shakes her head, holding back tears. "We went two days ago to meet him on the bus, and he never got off."

"Well, do they know where he's at?"

She shakes her head and gives in to the tears.

My mom comes downstairs at that second, takes one look at a broken-down Ercita, and turns to me. I quickly tell her what she just said.

Mom walks over and wraps her arms around Ercita. "It's okay." She sits with her on the couch. "When was the last time you spoke to your brother?"

"A week ago." She sniffs. "He'd already crossed the border into America."

Mom nods, in full-on investigator role. "Good. Did you use the same sponsor you used for your sister and mother?"

Ercita shakes her head. "No, we used a new one. But he came highly recommended."

"By whom?"

"Other people in our apartments that have used him."

Mom hands her a tissue. "Name?"

"Lynn Hoppman."

Mentally I catalog that name.

Mom gets up. "Let me make some phone calls."

Ercita nods, and Mom charges off into her office. "Lane, make sure your brother's up," she says right before closing the door.

I get up from the table and go upstairs. I'm eager to research Lynn Hoppman. My inner sense tells me something's up. I'm curious to find out what. . . .

Chapter Seventeen

FIRST-PERIOD TA JOB I DO MY CUSTOMARY checking in with Mr. Bealles, then head over to my station. Reggie calls me not more than five minutes later.

"Got your message. What happened?"

"Nothing to worry about." I continue the lie. "Like I said, I got in trouble with Mom. You covered your tracks, right? I don't want the FBI to know I got nosy in their Decapitator business and you helped me." I don't want the Decapitator to know my best friend helped me research him.

Reggie snorts. "Puh-lease. Did you just meet me? Nobody knows anything I do. I have so many filters it would take two of me just to figure me out."

I like it when Reggie gets cocky. "You sure?"

"I'm positive."

I believe her. But I'm still not taking any chances. "You're a good friend, Reg, but no more on the Decapitator. Okay?"

"Yeah, yeah, yeah."

I don't press it. I know if I do she'll pick up on my tone, so I play it cool. "Be a good girl."

She laughs at that and hangs up. What I need to do is give her something to sidetrack her. Something non–serial killer. Something harmless. I'll get her involved with researching Lynn Hoppman when I know a little more.

I log on to the computer, disable the wireless, and plug in my flash drive. I bring up the Decapitator files Reggie sent me and begin perusing them. Each of the known victims was a blonde and a preschool teacher. Two points of similarity. They don't share the same names or birthdates. And since the killer has moved around, they're certainly not from the same area.

Blond and preschool teachers. The kill month of September is a common detail as well, but with the skipping of years . . .

Maybe he didn't skip years. Maybe the blond hair is a key. A lot of women color their hair. Perhaps that's why certain kills aren't linked, because the victim had changed their hair color to a brunette or a redhead.

The thing, though, is that the location varies. Some are found in homes, others in warehouses. One was done with a chainsaw, others with electric carvers, and yet others with butcher knives.

The guy's good, or he's really stupid.

My gut tells me he's good, mixed with the other.

Somehow the killer has got to be connected to the preschool-teacher detail. This is his preference, and there's got to be a reason why.

Back to me and how I fit into all this. He's "chosen" me for a reason. I am none of his things, though. I'm not a blonde, fake or real, and the last thing I ever want to be is a preschool teacher. September has no significance to me, and none of the victims have ever been as young as me. The Decapitator doesn't want to kill me. He's involving me for some other reason.

I focus back on the files Reggie has sent. She's included several profiles put together over the years. At first the experts thought the killer was a teacher at the same school. Then after the second kill the experts thought it might be a copycat. The third kill occurred, and the experts concluded it was a middle-aged man, intelligent, financially secure, personable, grieving the loss of a loved one.

Hacking someone apart with a knife is an interesting way to grieve the loss of a loved one.

If I were grieving for a family member, I would visit their grave and put flowers on it.

Or maybe I wouldn't. Maybe I'd just stare at their picture

and remember different times. I guess I've never thought about it. I really don't know what type of griever I'd be.

Will I cry when/if my parents die? I didn't grieve for my real dad. I wasn't even born when he passed. I don't remember any of it. Anyway, the way I'm going, I'll die before my mom and stepdad, most likely.

I glance at the clock on the wall. I have fifteen minutes. Time enough to quickly research Lynn Hoppman. I take my flash drive out, re-enable the wireless, and type in Lynn's name.

"Who's Lynn Hoppman?"

I glance over my shoulder to Zach. That's twice in one day I've been "caught." First with Victor and the leg and now this.

In one swift movement I stand, grab Zach's wrist, and pull him between two tall bookshelves.

I back him up against one and go straight for his mouth. He tastes like a mixture of orange juice and doughnuts, and somewhere in the back of my brain I wonder what I taste like.

It must be good because he hungrily responds, running his hands all over my butt, my breasts, my body. I reach for the snap of his jeans.

"Whoa," he whispers, stilling my hands.

I'm just trying to reciprocate. What's the problem? I brush my fingers over his hard-on and he sucks in some air.

"O-kay." Gently he pushes me away. "Believe me, I so want this to go where you're directing it. But"—he laughs—"we're in the library, the bell's about to ring, and"—he glances down at his protruding jeans—"I suddenly need a cold shower."

I tune in to my aroused body and want . . . something . . . *now*. I reach for his hand and put it between my legs. His eyes go wide. I push his hand into me, rotate my hips, rotate them again, and my whole body rolls with a spasm. I stare right into his brown eyes that look so much like Dr. Issa's as I ride the wave.

"God damn," he breathes.

A heartbeat passes and I swallow. "We need to do this again sometime."

He doesn't respond as I walk back to my computer, log off, and gather my things.

The bell rings, and I glance back to the bookcases to see Zach still standing there looking at me.

If we have a repeat performance, will I think of Dr. Issa again?

Chapter Eighteen

LYNN HOPPMAN LIVES IN A BIG EFFING house on the Potomac. He is a financial planner with clients all over the world. He is not married and does not have any children. I have no clue what he does with such a big house if he's all alone. And from everything me and Google found out, the guy's clean. So I pick up the phone and dial Reggie.

"Yo." She greets me in her customary way.

"So Ercita, our housekeeper . . ." I go right into things, quickly giving Reggie the rundown on what's happened. "Mom's helping a little, but honestly, she's so overwhelmed with her normal work I don't know how much she can assist. I told Ercita I'd help her by finding out about this Lynn guy. But he's coming up clean. Can you do your digging magic?" Of course I didn't tell Ercita I'd help, but Reggie doesn't need to know that.

"Sure. Let me see what I can find."

"Thanks." I leave out the part that I plan on handling Lynn myself if he turns out to be the deviant my inner sense thinks he is.

"Everything going to be okay with Ercita?" I ask my mom over dinner Tuesday night.

She sighs. "I don't know. I've got some friends working on it."

"What about that man she mentioned. Lee"—I purposefully misname him—"somebody?"

"Lynn Hoppman," my mom says. "He checks out clean. Ercita was right. He's successfully helped numerous people come to America on work visas."

"Hm."

Later, after dinner, I give my standard going-to-study-at-the-coffee-house line and head to Lynn's mansion.

Between a security gate and perimeter fencing there's no getting in.

I park down the road, where I can scope out his comings and goings. It might be a while, so I get my calculus homework out and dive in.

A little over an hour later a Jaguar pulls up to the gate; the driver punches a code and rolls on in. Lynn Hoppman's home from work.

Using my binoculars, I check out as much as I can, but with the property's surrounding thick trees it's impossible. I could rent a kayak and laze my way right down the river his property overlooks, but frankly I don't want to get some funky infection.

The Potomac isn't known for its cleanliness.

Another thirty minutes tick by, and he comes back out in his Jaguar. I guess he's not home for the evening after all. I follow a safe distance behind as he heads into DC.

He makes a stop for wine and eventually finds his way to a condo off Connecticut Avenue NW. He feeds a meter and turns toward the building.

"Lynn!" a guy yells from a balcony four stories up.

Lynn holds the paper bag in the air. "Got the pinot you wanted."

The guy waves. "Come on up."

Lynn disappears into the building and a few minutes later reappears on the balcony with the guy. They uncork the wine, pour two glasses, and settle down to visit.

My cell chimes Reggie's personalized ring. "Whatcha got?" I answer.

"Hoppman's clean. Can't find anything. Except . . ."

I wait. Reggie sometimes has a penchant for drama.

"His father owned a warehouse in Fairfax. Hoppman inherited it when the father died. He donated the property to a nonprofit that moved its headquarters to Rockville."

"So the warehouse is sitting empty?" I surmise.

"And because it's changed hands several times, there's quite a paper trail. However, someone with my expert hacking skills saw it as a mild challenge."

I can just imagine her swag expression on the other end. "Anything else?"

"Nope."

"Thanks. I'll pass it along to Mom and Ercita," I fib.

"Okeydoke. Bye."

She texts me the address and I set my GPS. I get a little lost, and an hour later I pull down a long gravel road bordered by trees and into an empty dirt parking lot. A dark, abandoned warehouse sits some fifty yards away surrounded by a chain-link fence.

I park for a few minutes and survey the vacant area. It's a small warehouse with old, faded graffiti decorating the metal walls. I'd say it's probably three thousand square feet. Certainly not the size of a Super Target, but big enough.

I look along the roofline but don't see any security cameras.

To the right of the warehouse sits a tractor-trailer.

I study the tall chain-link fence, zeroing in on the barbed wire along the top. Interesting. Clearly, Lynn doesn't want people getting in or out.

I roll my window down and tune my ears in to the night. Crickets chirp in the nearby trees. Car engines rev by up on the highway. Industrial fans in the warehouse's roof whirl.

Anybody coming down the gravel road would see me sitting here. Not good.

I glance around through the darkness and eye the nearby woods. I put my Wrangler in four-wheel drive and head straight for a gap in the trees.

I drive far enough in to be hidden, cut my engine, sit, and wait.

I'm good at waiting. Always have been. I have a lot of patience. I'm that kid parents take to church, and while all the other kids have to go to the children's service, I get to stay in the congregation with the adults.

Not that I've been to church tons, but my parents have taken us a few times.

About an hour in I decide nothing's going to happen and go to crank my engine, but then I catch headlights glowing down the gravel road.

Seconds later a truck comes into view. It drives right past me and up to the chain-link fence. Lynn Hoppman gets out. He unlocks the fence and drives through.

Somewhere between the boyfriend on Connecticut and here he's changed vehicles.

He parks his truck next to the tractor-trailer, climbs in, and starts it up. He pulls a gun from the waistband of his jeans and approaches the warehouse. *A gun?*

Something's going down, and I don't have everything I need. I do have my Taser, my face mask, and gloves, but I'm not wearing the right clothes, I don't have any zip ties, nor did I bring tranquilizer. Oh, and he's got a *gun*!

Okay, focus. There's no way I'm turning back. I *will* go forward. I will keep my wits about myself, focus on disarming him, and, while staying conscious of the bullets, block them out. If there's anything that aikido has taught me, it is the ability to compartmentalize.

Starting tomorrow I'll always be prepared. This right now proves I can't plan all my attacks.

I lower the ski mask over my head and face, slip my gloves on, and jump from the Jeep.

I sprint across the dirt parking lot, straight through the open gate, and around the side of the warehouse where the tractor-trailer sits idling. I merge into the shadows and flatten my back against the warehouse's metal wall.

Maintain focus. Stay calm.

In aikido I have been trained to be the defender, not the attacker. *Tonight. I. Am. The. Attacker.* Power fills me, and I silently recite that one more time. *Tonight. I. Am. The. Attacker.*

"Move!" barks a voice from around the side of the warehouse.

A second later a young girl steps from the corner, then an older teen, and then a man I'd put in his early twenties. Their mouths are duct-taped shut, and their wrists are secured behind their backs.

The young girl glances over, and her tear-filled eyes widen

when she sees me. I shake my head and hold a finger to my mouth. *Shhh.*

Lynn Hoppman appears then, the gun held out, pointed at the three captives.

I'm already off his line of force, and I move, grabbing the gun barrel with my left hand and his wrist with my right. The gun goes off, and its booming release surges through my ears as I jerk away. Lynn whips around and lands a solid punch on my jaw. The impact shocks me off-balance and sends me stumbling backward. Adrenaline spikes through my veins, fueling me with anger, and propels me forward.

I lunge and grab the gun, press and twist it free, bring the barrel back, and strike him once in the head. Not giving him a chance to regain balance, I go straight into a circular throw, changing directions, and spinning him around.

His face hits the concrete. He rolls over and throws a kick, and it lands solidly on my shin. *Son of a bitch!* Panic spears fury through me that's he's one up. I channel its energy into slamming the gun against the side of his head. Blood squirts out and immediately fills the air with a coppery scent. My nostrils flare in primal response at the sight and smell.

I lock his arm and press my thumb into the concavity behind his left ear. His body sinks lifeless in a brief loss of consciousness. I almost sink with him in relief. *Not yet, Lane. Move!* Quickly I run over to the truck he'd driven in and leap into the bed. I flip open the large toolbox, rifle through, find duct tape, and snatch it up.

Lynn Hoppman groans and sluggishly tries to get up. I jump from the truck, cover the ground back to him, and jab my knee between his fifth and sixth thoracic vertebrae.

I twist both wrists back and duct-tape them together, lever up and do his legs, then slam the gun into his head again. This time when blood squirts, I smile.

Finally I turn to the three captives.

What the hell am I going to do with them?

Lynn moans and lets out a string of curses, and I swipe the duct tape over his mouth. I search his pockets and find keys and a phone.

I dial 911, and through my mask I lower my voice for disguise. "Lynn Hoppman. Fifteen Carmel Lane, Fairfax. Three people hostage."

Leaving the phone on, I put it, the keys, and the gun on the ground beside the truck. The gun . . . I eye it for a second, considering . . . I can easily kill him, and that powerful thought straightens my spine. His life sits in my hands. But . . . does he deserve that finality? No, I can't see that he does. He deserves to suffer, for sure. Just like he made others suffer.

In my peripheral vision I see one of the captives move, and I spin around. They're all staring at me with relief and fear in their eyes.

Fear? But I'm here to help them.

I peel the tape off their mouths.

"Por favor, ayúdeme," the young girl pleads.

I make a quick decision to leave them tied up. I need to get out of here, and I can't afford them either following me or trying to keep me here.

"It's okay," the twenty-something guy says with a thick accent. *Federico?* "Get out of here. Help's on the way."

I nod and take off into the night. In my Jeep I crank the engine and four-wheel out of the woods and down the gravel road. I don't turn my lights on, and trust the darkness will provide me with the necessary cover.

I tug the mask from my head as I reach the end of the gravel road. I turn onto the county highway and flip my lights on, and police sirens echo in the distance. What a rush. What a great big effing rush. The gun, being hit, almost losing it, the adrenaline, the relief . . . the blood. Seeing it squirt. *Oh* . . . that was amazing.

A half mile later four squad cars whip past me.

A half mile after that so does an ambulance.

Lynn Hoppman's about to get everything he deserves. And that fills me with a different type of rush. Another wrong righted. *Slim justice.*

The gun . . . I could've easily killed him, and yet I chose not to. I think I'm discovering it might not be necessary. But can I truly fulfill my darkest urges without the finality of death?

Chapter Nineteen

IT'S ALL OVER THE NEWS THE NEXT DAY.

Mom nods to the TV. "Did you hear Ercita's brother Federico was part of that?"

I shake my head. "What was that man going to do with them?"

"Sell them into sex slavery."

My stomach clenches. What a horrible man. Maybe I *should* have killed him.

Gently Mom touches the yellow bruise on my chin where Lynn hit me. "Aikido?"

I nod. I've had bruises before, so one on my chin is really no big deal.

I tune back in to the TV and watch as the camera goes

inside the warehouse to show dirty blankets on the floor, a bucket for urine in the corner, and several rats scurrying about. The reporter starts in on the description of the person who rescued the captives and ends with, "It looks like the Masked Savior has struck again."

Justin shovels in a bite of cereal. "It's like we have our own superhero."

"Oh, please," Daisy snorts. "Masked Savior. How stupid."

This is one thing I agree on with Daisy.

Later at school Zach finds me in the hall. "So . . . *crazy* what happened between us in the library."

"Yes, crazy," I answer, only because I think that's what he wants to hear.

He waits for me to say more, but I don't.

"Well, anyway. It's interesting you were googling Lynn Hoppman, and then he's all over the news this morning."

Seeing as how we're in a crowded hall, I can't use sex to distract him this time. So I agree, "Yeah, it is strange."

"Why *were* you researching him?"

See, this is the thing. He thinks because we made out he can ask me whatever he wants. I don't agree. My business is my business and his is his. If I wanted to *share*, I would. However, I don't. This is not polite communication, though, so I say instead, "The lady who cleans our house . . ."

And I go on to tell him about Ercita and my mom helping,

dropping major hints the FBI likely had a lot to do with the whole thing.

"That's really great of your mom," he comments, his curiosity seemingly alleviated.

The whole thing only serves as a reminder I need to be more careful.

That afternoon I check the news feeds to see a sketch artist has put together a depiction of the Masked Savior. He is tall and skinny. He dresses in all black. He wears a full-face mask. Some sketches are even showing me with a cape. Justin will like that.

But thanks to my flat chest, deep voice, and tomboy stride, Lynn Hoppman's captives in no way guessed I'm a girl.

Good.

I'm working a midweek shift at Patch and Paw and head over after school.

I go straight to boarding and find Corn Chip absent.

"He'll be here this weekend," the receptionist tells me. "That other cute one's here. What's his name? Bear. That white Bichon?"

"Thanks," I mumble.

True, Bear's cute, but he doesn't do it for me. Visiting with Corn Chip always brings my world back into focus. There's just something about his knowing, dark stare and bushy gray brows. They have this way of cocking right and left when he's looking at me. Even when I'm not talking, he seems to know what I'm thinking.

I look through the list of things that need to be done and choose trays first. After collecting all of them from the kitty condos I head out back to wash and disinfect them.

Tonight I'll check the nanny cam and see if I've missed anything. I also want to try accessing Mom's computer. I've attempted before and failed, but one never knows. It's worth a go again. Because surely she's got to have files that will help me connect the Decapitator dots and figure out why he's contacted me directly.

I sense more than hear someone behind me and turn to see Dr. Issa. He gives me that shy, intelligent smile that does weird things to my insides. I haven't seen him since the kiss and am curious to see if he'll bring it up.

"Heard you and Daniel, or rather Zach, are dating," he begins.

Dating? I don't consider us dating. We went to hockey and made out. "We went to a hockey game." I leave out the part where we swallowed tongues and he gave me an orgasm in the library.

"Um," Dr. Issa looks down. "How about we forget what happened between us? You're a nice girl and all, but—"

"Okay."

He looks at me. "Okay?"

I shrug and tell myself I don't care. Really, what's the point anyway? Emotional attachment, talking things out, drama. If more people will just say what they mean, accept and move on, then life can cruise along at a steady unencumbered clip. Why don't more people realize this?

Yes, I tell myself this as I look him straight in his adorable eyes.

"Oh." Dr. Issa just stands there a second.

I wait. "Anything else?"

With a shake of his head he reaches for the door, then, as a second thought, turns back to me. "Lane, I don't think I've ever met anyone like you."

I've been told this before. And I never know what to say in return, so I maintain eye contact and wait for whatever comes next.

He sighs. "I'm going home for the night." But he doesn't move.

"Was that a compliment?"

He laughs. "I'm not sure what it was."

I decide to bring up the other night. "I saw your Juke at Target in Seven Corners."

"I live near there." He turns back to the door.

"Mom said she saw you buying home improvement stuff?"

He doesn't look at me when he answers, "Yes, that's right. See you later." And with that he's gone.

I don't know why I'm questioning Dr. Issa about shopping. It's really none of my business what he does or doesn't buy in Target.

At nine o'clock I'm the last one out. I lock up and head to my Jeep. A yellow piece of paper stuck under my wiper catches my attention. I look around the dark parking lot. *He's contacted me again.* I round the driver's side and see a long, deep, jagged white mark where someone's keyed my Wrangler. It strikes me as odd that the Decapitator would do such a thing.

I open the yellow piece of paper and read: *Stay away from Zach.*

No, this isn't the Decapitator. This is an ex-girlfriend. I'll bet anything. I grab my phone and text Zach. MEET ME?

SURE, he immediately types back. U AT P&P?

YES, I answer. I'LL WAIT HERE.

Ten minutes later he pulls in. "Oh, dammit all to hell," is what he says when he sees my keyed Jeep.

I hand him the note and watch him read it.

He frowns. "She's done this before."

"She?"

"My ex-girlfriend."

"She makes a habit out of keying people's cars?"

Zach gives a guilty cringe.

I thought as much. And I don't want anything to do with deranged exes. "I don't do this, Zach." I tap the yellow piece of paper. "This has officially made things difficult between you and me."

Zach takes on a look of panic. "Lane . . ."

I climb into my Wrangler.

"Lane." He takes a step toward me. "Wait."

I give him a friendly look. There's no reason why I have to be mean. "I'll see you around, Zach, okay?"

He doesn't answer at first. I don't want to hurt him. But like I said, this isn't me. I don't do this kind of stuff. I don't do drama.

Zach moves back. "Yeah, see you around."

Without a glance in his direction, I pull from the parking lot. I've got too much going on right now. If things with Zach can't be simple, then sadly there can't be a "things with Zach." Although I could use another library encounter. . . .

When I get home, I set the house alarm, grab my mail off the kitchen counter, and head straight up to my bedroom. I shuffle through mostly junk mail, and tucked in the middle is a small white envelope. The Decapitator has sent me something again.

My stomach muscles clench in anticipation as I carefully break the seal and slide the card out.

Friday. Midnight.
4 Buchold Place
Herndon

Immediately I flip the card over, and sure enough, on the back is another picture. But this one is a shot of Daisy sitting with her friends at an outdoor café. Below it is typed:

**TELL ANYONE AND I *WILL* HURT YOU.
I *WILL* GO AFTER YOUR FAMILY.**

What? My family? How dare he! Threaten me and it's one thing, but my family . . . my mom, my sister, my brother . . .

Anger rolls through me as I read and reread that last line. Oh, he's picked the wrong unbalanced person to threaten. He's going to figure that out real quick.

I'm disgusted with myself for even being minutely fascinated with this evil man. What was I thinking? My family. Son of a bitch—you don't mess with my family!

I'm not scared of him; I'm infuriated. He's pissed me off. I'm going to carve him up just like he sliced all those innocent people. I *will* kill him.

I pace across my room, my jaw clenched, telling myself to calm down and at the same time welcoming the rage filling my body. Rage is good, and when mixed with focus, very powerful.

Friday. Midnight. He either wants me to find the next body part, or he wants to meet me. I can't imagine he just wants to meet me, unless he somehow knows I'm the Masked Savior. And why would he care one way or the other if I am, unless he imagines there's some similarity between us?

Unless . . . a shiver of terror runs down my spine as a new thought forms.

Do I already know him?

Chapter Twenty

FOUR BUCHOLD PLACE CONSUMES MY EVERY thought the entire next day at school. I look the address up and get nowhere. I check Google Maps, but the trees prohibit an accurate satellite image. My natural inclination is to ask Reggie for help, and so I pick up the phone.

"Yo. Everything work out okay with that Lynn Hoppman information?"

Sometimes I forget she's in Massachusetts and not privy to local news. I quickly give her the rundown.

"Wow. How crazy. I'm so glad my information helped."

"Me too. Hey, listen, do you have time to look something up for me?"

"Sure. What's up?"

"I was looking through an old scrapbook"—I start the lie—
"and saw an envelope marked with an address in Herndon,
Virginia. I looked it up and can't really figure out who lives or
lived there. Mind doing some digging?"

"Why don't you just ask your mom?"

"She's so busy with work," I say. "I don't want to bother her.
Listen, if you don't have time, it's really no big deal. . . ."

"Please, you know I'm the queen of multitasking. I always
have time. I'll look it up. It's probably some old relative or something."

"Probably."

We hang up; I text Reggie the address and start making
a mental list. Taser. Zip ties. Gloves. Ski mask. Cargo pants.
Tranquilizer.

Tranquilizer. I'll have to stop by Patch and Paw and steal
some. I'll wait until six o'clock. That's when the shift changes—
people come and go, and I'll be least likely to be noticed in the
stockroom.

"Hey, Slim."

I snap out of my zone and look up at the president of the
science club passing me by in the cafeteria. I give him a nod, go
to dump my garbage, and see Zach sitting off by himself.

His hunched shoulders, drooped head, and picking-at-his-
food demeanor have me walking toward him.

I sit down beside him but don't say a word.

He doesn't even spare me a glance. "I almost tipped up a bottle of rum last night," he admits.

My heart sinks. "Zach," I start.

"It's not because of you, so don't go feeling guilty or anything." He pushes his lunch tray away. "My ex-girlfriend, Belinda, and I used to get drunk together. *All* the time. When I voluntarily went into rehab, it's like it offended her or something. She visited me once, doing the 'good girlfriend' thing, and then never came back."

I don't know what to say, so I focus on being a good listener.

"I learned a lot about myself in rehab. What's healthy. What's not. Anyway, I broke up with her, and let's just say she's not the nicest of drunks. What she did to your Jeep is a very small portion of what she's capable of. She's the reason why I chose not to go back to private school."

He lets out a laugh that holds no amusement. "And she used to be the nicest girl."

I can take care of her, I almost suggest, but instead I ask, "When did you notice she had a dark side?"

He finally glances over at me. "Hm. I've never thought about her as 'dark.'"

I ignore that. "Do you think she was born dark, or do you think she became dark?"

Zach gives that a lot of consideration. "I think she became dark."

Or maybe Belinda was born dark and has hidden it well.

Around six o'clock I stop into Patch and Paw.

"What are you doing here?" the receptionist asks.

"Forgot my travel mug." I head past her and into the back. The usual stuff is going on—last-minute appointments, people cleaning, others packing up to head home.

I stroll straight into the storage closet and over to the tranquilizers. I don't hesitate as I reach up and snag a vial. I'm beginning to question the idea of using a sedative to end a person's life. It's clean but holds no significance for me.

The serial killers I've studied use the same method time and again. A method they not only choose but that chooses them as well.

If I'm meant to be a killer, I'll find my method. I can't force it. It has to happen naturally. This I know.

After pocketing the vial, I head back out to my Jeep. Across the parking lot stands Dr. Issa and a dark-haired woman. I can't hear what they're saying, but they're obviously arguing.

She climbs into her white Prius and peels out of the parking lot. Dr. Issa turns and kicks the tire on his Juke. I blink in surprise. I've never seen him angry.

He kicks it one more time, turns, catches sight of me, and hesitates.

A few seconds later he gives me a nod, strolls the long way around the lot, and back into Patch and Paw.

I've never experienced jealousy before. It has never been an issue for me. But I'm jealous of the dark-haired woman, even if they've been arguing. It's unsettling to admit that to myself. I always considered that emotion beneath my common sense.

By Friday I still haven't heard from Reggie about 4 Buchold Place. My day is usual. Morning coffee, school, Daisy heading off for a Friday date, me taking Justin to aikido. Me thinking nonstop about the big event tonight.

By seven p.m. I'm back home. Victor and Mom order pizza. At nine p.m. I ask if I can catch a late movie. They don't mind as long as I'm home by curfew. But since the Decapitator wants to meet at midnight, I already know I'll break curfew, which I've never done before.

By eleven p.m. I'm sitting down the road from 4 Buchold Place. I know I'm way early, but curiosity has more than won out.

It's a small redbrick house. Dark. Unkempt. Doesn't look like anyone's lived in it for years. But the grass isn't too high, so obviously someone has.

Large oak trees overwhelm the front, the sides, and the

backyard. Their limbs extend out and touch each other to form a canopy over the small property. No wonder Google Maps gave me squat.

Up and down Buchold Place houses similar to this one dot the lots. Some of them are unkempt as well, making number four blend in just fine.

11:15. I check my cell phone. Still nothing from Reggie.

11:30. I pack my cargo pants with my supplies.

11:45. I tuck my hair inside the ski mask.

11:50. I give the dark street one last survey and reach for the door.

My cell chimes. Reggie has the worst timing.

"Better be good," I answer.

"Four Buchold Place belongs to your father. Your *real* dad, not your stepdad."

My whole body goes numb. "Reggie, my *real* father is dead."

"No. He's not."

What?

Chapter Twenty-One

I DON'T GO INTO 4 BUCHOLD PLACE AT midnight. I turn around and go home. No one even knows I've broken curfew.

I don't know what is waiting for me in number four. What I do know is that my mom lied to me.

The next morning I call Reggie. "Can you hack into my mom's computer?"

Silence.

I already know the answer. For Reggie, my mom's off-limits. Sometimes I think she admires and respects Mom more than I do. Reggie and Mom met the same summer we became friends at camp. I think Mom must have sensed Reggie's sadness, because she gave my friend her e-mail address and told her to message any time. Reggie did about six months later. I don't have a problem with their surrogate mother/daughter relationship. I know Reggie desperately needs a "real" parent after the crappy upbringing she had.

Reggie interrupts my thoughts. "You know I won't."

"I know." I sigh. "It was worth asking."

"Just ask her. I'm sure there's a perfectly logical explanation as to why she's not told you the truth."

Reggie's right. I need to talk to Mom.

The doorbell rings, and I glance at my bedside clock. Who'd be here at eight a.m. on a Saturday morning?

"Lane!" Victor yells up. "For you."

I hang up with Reggie and go downstairs. There's a short black girl standing at my door.

"Yes?" I say.

She smiles. "Are you Lane?"

I nod. Obviously or I wouldn't have been called down.

"I'm Belinda," she tells me, and waits like I'm supposed to know who she is. "Zach's girlfriend?" She laughs. "Or ex-girlfriend, I should say."

The delinquent who keyed my car. Lovely.

The differences between us are almost ridiculous. She is just as short as I am tall, as black as I am white, and all smiles where I am anything but.

Her smile grows even larger. "I wanted to meet you."

KILLER INSTINCT

"Why?"

She laughs again. "Any friend of Zach's is a friend of mine."

"I don't want to be your friend."

Her smile doesn't falter. "Okay, then. At least we met."

"That we did," I agree.

"So, are you and Zach planning on going to the football game?"

Football game? I don't go to football games. That's Daisy's scene. "Listen, I said I don't want to be your friend."

"That's fine, but you can at least be civil and answer my question."

"No, I can't. Good-bye." I close the door in her face.

"She seems nice," Victor cautiously comments.

"Don't let that act fool you."

"You could've been a little friendlier."

I flip the lock on our door. "Have you seen my keyed Jeep?"

He nods.

"She did that."

He sighs. "What's her name? I'm going to call her parents."

"Please let me handle this. Trust me?"

He doesn't immediately respond. Then, "Okay. I'll give you thirty days. If she hasn't made right her wrongs, I'm contacting her parents. Fair?"

"Fair." This is the good thing about my parents. They really *do* trust me.

125

Daisy comes down the stairs dressed in her cheerleading warm-ups. "Who's the chick?"

I go to the coffee. "Friend of Zach's."

"What's she want with you?"

"To say hi."

Victor grabs his keys. "Let's go, Daisy."

I pour milk into my mug as he and my sister head out to her Saturday cheerleading camp.

Mom comes downstairs. "Morning."

"Good morning." I take my first sip and watch her putter around the kitchen.

How to bring up my real dad circles around in my brain. I can't ask her about 4 Buchold Place because then I'll have to explain how I know about the address. And what am I supposed to say?

Mom, the Decapitator has been communicating with me, and I think he wanted to meet me last night at Four Buchold Place?

"Tell me about Dad," I say instead, giving her a chance to come clean with the lie. "My *real* dad."

She doesn't miss an FBI-trained beat. "Why do you ask?"

"Been studying about family trees in school," I say. "And it got me thinking. . . ."

Mom opens the bacon and starts laying it out on the skillet. "We met in the marines at Quantico. I got pregnant with you.

We never married. Before I even had a chance to tell him I was pregnant, he was killed while kayaking."

These are all the things she's told me before. "Mom, every time I bring him up, you tell me the exact same things. Please give me some solid details."

Mom grabs tongs and turns to me. "He was handsome. Intelligent. Liked to play golf. Dry sense of humor. Quiet man. Tall. Red hair."

"What attracted you to him?"

Mom smiles. "Great listener. True listener. One of those people who look deeply into your eyes and absorb every word you're saying."

I sip some more. "How did you all wind up together?"

Mom goes back to the bacon and flips a few. A bit of grease pops out. "He'd recently lost his dad, and I'd broken up with a boyfriend. We comforted each other. He had to go home to deal with family stuff and never came back. I found out later about the kayaking accident."

"He's buried in Oregon, right?" *More important, are you sure he's actually dead and buried?*

"Yes, in Oregon, next to his parents."

Oregon . . . Wait a minute, that's where one of the decapitations occurred. "Did you both live on base?" *Come on, Mom, mention 4 Buchold Place.*

"We had separate places."

"And he had no other family, right?"

"Right." Mom's cell conveniently buzzes and she checks it. "Watch the bacon for me," she tells me, and heads to her office.

Worst-case scenario: My real dad is alive, is the Decapitator, and wants to meet me.

Best-case scenario: My real dad is dead, someone else is the Decapitator, and I'm normal.

I spent my whole life thinking something in the environment made me into who I am, but if my real dad is the Decapitator, then I inherited this darkness in me.

Oh. My. God.

ANY LUCK W/ MOM? Reggie interrupts my panicked thought.

NO.

SORRY, BUT I'M NOT HACKING HER PC!

I KNOW . . .

WANT ME 2 DIG INTO DAD? she offers.

YES, I immediately type back. Clearly, it's the only way I'm going to find something out.

I turn the heat down on the bacon and stand for a second, digesting: *If my real dad is the Decapitator, then I inherited this darkness in me.* I can't quite wrap my brain around that enormous thought. This changes everything I've ever thought about myself.

My mom charges out of her office and straight over to the TV. She flips it on, and scrolling across the bottom is:

DECAPITATOR CAUGHT. DETAILS TO FOLLOW.

Wait a minute! What?

She snatches her purse up, making it more than obvious she's irritated. "I swear, you'd think with me being the lead on this case someone would contact me *before* it hits the news."

"Maybe you should sleep at headquarters until this is all over. So you don't miss anything else."

"That's not a half-bad idea." She motions to the bacon. "Got that? I won't be home till late."

I nod. "Justin and I'll be fine."

She races out and I turn back to the TV. *This can't be. How does this even make sense?*

Chapter Twenty-Two

BY MONDAY IT'S ALL OVER THE NEWS.

DECAPITATOR CAUGHT!

His name is James Donner. He is from Alaska. He is sixty-five years old and works as a traveling plumber. He has proof he lived in each state where the serial decapitations occurred.

He commits the crimes only once a year in September to mourn the loss of his wife, who was brutally murdered by a man who hacked her up with a knife.

His wife had been blond and worked as a preschool teacher. This, of course, explains how James picks his victims.

He's textbook.

Too perfect if you ask me.

The question from every reporter: *Why turn yourself in now?*

James Donner's response: *It was time.*

Personally I'm just relieved it's not my real father.

I've been researching James Donner pretty much nonstop since he came forward. If he truly is the Decapitator, then I should be connected to him in some way. Otherwise why send me the messages?

And why when I look at his image don't I sense some sort of link?

I'm dying to know what my mom thinks. What the FBI thinks.

The girl sitting beside me redirects my attention when I hear her say, "You know all those flyers that were hanging up for the missing cocker spaniel? I heard the guy that took it is that disturbed dude. He lives a few blocks over. What's his name?"

"Marco? Ugh. He's awful."

I tune in to their conversation. We have a substitute today in AP English, and she's letting us do pretty much whatever.

"He went to school here," the first girl says.

"Didn't he get expelled?" the second girl asks.

Marco. I remember him. Senior when I was a sophomore. *Did* get expelled for bringing a knife on campus. I thought he was in jail for mistreatment of animals. Clearly, I thought wrong.

"He carved some weird Nazi symbol in the cocker spaniel's back."

The second girl gasps. "A swastika? Is the dog okay?"

"Poor thing had to have stitches."

I'd hunt Marco down and kill him if he did that to Corn Chip.

"And then," the first girl goes on, "did you hear what he did to that cat?"

Second girl groans. "No."

"Cut off its tail."

"No!" second girl cries.

First girl shakes her head. "Slim remembers him. Don't ya, Slim?"

I nod. "I do."

First girl laughs. "Didn't your sister go out with him?"

God, I hope not. "Don't think so."

"Well," second girl chimes in, "someone needs to carve a swastika in *his* back. Let *him* see how it feels."

The bell rings and everyone files out. I go to my locker and grab my things. *Marco Morales.* I make a mental note as the familiar craving crawls just below my skin. I'm going to find out where this guy lives. Yes, I'm *definitely* going to find out about this guy.

"Hey, you." Zach comes up beside me.

"Hey."

"Wanted to let you know I talked to my ex-girlfriend, and she's not going to give you any more problems."

I don't bother telling him she came to my house. "Okay."

"So, we good?"

"We're good." We've always "been good" as far as I'm concerned, but whatever he needs to hear, I guess.

I close my locker and spin the lock. Zach follows me out to student parking, and I immediately notice the temp has changed throughout the day to a cooler breeze.

"Kind of anticlimactic with that Donner guy turning himself in, huh?"

I'll say.

Daisy comes up beside us, holding hands with her latest. "West is going to take me home," she tells me, glancing at Zach and snuggling into West like she's trying to make Zach jealous.

After you provide him with your outstanding fellatio services? I want to ask, but nod my head instead. On a thought, I stop her. "Hey, did you date a Marco?"

She fakes a blush. "No."

Not that she'd tell me if she did, at least not in front of the guys. Daisy's the queen of making guys think she's innocent.

West tugs her hand, and they head off in one direction. Zach gives me a wave and heads off in another, and I go toward my Jeep.

I always park at the far end of the lot near the entrance so it's easy to get out in the afternoons. It's a long walk but worth it not to have to wait idle in a car line.

As I unlock my Wrangler, a shadow moves, and I glance over my shoulder to see Belinda. She doesn't even go to school here. What is she doing?

I turn fully to face her. She's not smiling, and in her gaze I see the *real* Belinda. Dark. Conniving. Controlling. Seeing her sparks a confident, focused energy in me that I welcome.

I'm fully aware the long line of students leaving campus can see us. Maybe she planned it this way. To stir up gossip. This'll be all over campus tomorrow. *Mysterious girl confronts Slim.*

"Maybe I didn't make myself clear," she begins. "Stay away from Zach."

Any friend of Zach's is a friend of mine, I want to remind her. "You're officially annoying me," I say instead.

She moves then, cocking her chest and face in my personal space.

I don't flinch. I don't move. But I do curve my lips into an uncustomary smile.

Belinda falters. "What do you think you're doing, *bitch*?"

"*I'm* not doing anything. *You're* the one who's approached me."

She sucks her teeth and gets right in my personal space again, this time bumping her chest to mine. "What are you going to do about it?"

Really? "Listen, you don't know me, but fair warning: You don't want to mess with me."

She tilts her head. "You think I'm scared of you?"

You should be, I want to say, but frankly I'm done. Let her try her piss-poor scare tactics on some other girl. It's not working on me.

She glances around the parking lot, probably trying to see if anyone's watching her little show. I wait until she turns back before I calmly trace my finger along the keyed line she made and then climb into my Wrangler. Without a glance in her direction, I crank the engine, put it in first, and do my customary cut in line to exit campus.

I could've told her Victor's going to call her parents if she doesn't fix my keyed Jeep, but that's a Daisy move. I like to handle my own problems.

Belinda is annoying me. But not enough to warrant my focus. For now, at least.

After I pick Justin up, we head home. He starts in on his homework, and I go to my room. I check the nanny-cam footage.

"Donner knows about the hands and feet." Mom is speaking into the phone. "We haven't released that information yet, but you never know with inside leaks."

Hands and feet? What about the hands and feet? They're missing from the arms and legs and get delivered later in a cooler. I know this from the other reports. So what are they talking about?

Mom listens for a minute. "Yes, I think he's faking that."

A couple more listening seconds go by and then she

responds, "So James Donner is either the real Decapitator or a very knowledgeable fake."

They move on to discuss something else, and I pull up the pictures I have of the arm thrown off the bridge and the leg from the ice rink. I pull up pictures of his past murders and confirm once again there are no hands or feet. What mysterious detail does James Donner know that I don't?

I dig into all the information Reggie sent me. I reread every police report from the past murders. It's always a head first, then an arm, a leg, the other arm, finished by the other leg. He ends by sending the hands and feet to the police department in a special delivery cooler.

Personally, if I was Mr. Donner, I would've waited to reveal myself by hand-delivering that cooler.

But I'm not Mr. Donner.

What I want to know is, what's going to happen to the arm and leg that have yet to be revealed? Maybe James Donner has prearranged their discovery. Or perhaps he's decided to leave their whereabouts a mystery. And 4 Buchold Place and me. There are too many loose ends here. If he's the true Decapitator, he's got to be connected to number four and me. He's just got to.

As I ponder this, I unload my book bag and mentally switch gears to Marco Morales. Tonight I'll head over to his address and see what he's up to. I need a good fix. I need to relieve the unfulfilled tension in me. Taking my frustration out on someone deserving like Marco is the perfect idea. Because I have no problem carving a swastika into his animal-torturing self. And if he had a tail, I'd have no problem cutting off that as well.

Which gives me an idea. . . .

I'm going to find out *exactly* what he's done to animals, and then . . . I smile. How much will I make him suffer in return?

Chapter Twenty-Three

ON TUESDAY EVENING I PULL INTO MARCO'S apartment complex, locate his number, and park nearby. He's sitting alone on his balcony, smoking, staring off into the woods. As I watch him my mind begins to wander.

The thing about most abusers is that they don't just become abusers. Something significant happens to them to make them into the person they are.

This, of course, does not hold true in every situation.

Look at Reggie, for example. Her dad slapped her around pretty much on a nightly basis. Granted, she now lives inside a computer and has only one friend, me, but she's never harmed another living thing. Nor will she ever.

Then there's the occasional abuser that's a mystery. They're raised in a loving home, never spanked, and likely given every-thing they ever wanted. Yet they turn out rotten.

What's the magic equation that produces the perfect per-son? I don't think there is one. I think each person is shaped by the events in their life and ultimately decides which way they want to go.

Take my family. Although I have a different father, all three of us kids have been raised by the same parents. Justin's about as perfect as they come. Daisy's a misguided missile. And I'm, well . . . I suppose I'm still trying to figure the ins and outs of that one.

I tried hypnosis once to find out more about why I am who I am and came out with nothing. With the new knowledge about my real dad, maybe it's time to do it again. There might just be some twisted memory stuck in the dark corners of my mind. Or . . . there might be nothing.

As far as Marco Morales, basically he had no parental supervision. His mom and dad are day laborers, working every job they can possibly pick up.

Marco's one of eight kids. The family's a perfect example of my point. Two of the kids studied hard and got college scholar-ships. One of the girls got pregnant at fifteen and is currently living on the government. Two, including Marco, have been in and out of trouble and jail. The remaining three are sprinkled between elementary and middle school.

"Fuck yeah, I'm going," Marco says into his phone, and I refocus in on him.

He takes a drag of a cigarette. "There's going to be ass all in that party."

Basically he's an idiot. I've been sitting here, boldly watching him for a while now, and he hasn't once glanced in my direction.

He crushes a beer can and grabs another from the twelve-pack sitting next to his plastic chair. Why guys feel the need to crush cans has always perplexed me. Maybe it's some primal show of testosterone.

One of his roommates comes out onto the balcony. "We're leaving. See you there?"

Marco nods and tosses the roommate a beer.

As he continues yapping his mouth into the phone, the roommates file out and into an old Chevy. Cranking their music to a thumping level, they slowly, badasslike, pull from the lot.

Posers.

I go back to looking at Marco. He hangs up the phone, crushes his already empty can, and starts on another. *Don't get too drunk, Mr. Marco. I want you good and awake for what's in store.*

From a first-story apartment saunters a cat, and I catch sight of it at the exact same second Marco does.

I watch as he watches it, and I can visualize his twisted brain devising a torturous plan.

"Here, kitty, kitty, kitty," he sweetly calls.

The cat lazily arches its back in an atypical show of interest, and my every nerve ending goes on alert. I swerve my gaze back up to Marco and stare as he reaches beneath his seat and pulls out a BB gun. He sights down the length at the cat, and I immediately slam my hand into my horn.

The cat scurries and Marco jumps.

A couple of seconds tick by. Marco laughs and, with his BB gun, heads inside.

I hop out of my Wrangler, and as I trot up his second-story apartment stairs, I lower the ski mask over my face. There's no place I'd rather be than right here, right now, making Marco pay for his depravities. I turn his door knob, take a brief second to enjoy the exhilaration bubbling through me, and then walk right inside.

My nostrils flare beneath my ski mask at the funky smell— like unclean feet and intestines.

As I listen to him peeing in the bathroom, I lock the door and look around his disgusting apartment. Days-old fast-food containers take up the kitchen counters. Bags of pot litter the coffee table. A dead roach lies in the corner. Suspicious stains dot the gray couches and tan-carpeted floor. Dirty boy underwear is looped over a chair's back.

Marco stumbles from the bathroom. I doubt he washed his hands.

"What the fuck?" he slurs.

I raise the Taser and pull the trigger. Barbs fly across the small space, and he dodges back into the bathroom.

Dammit.

I race after him and round the corner, and he sprays something in my face. "Aarrgghh!" I stumble back and he comes at me. Through my hazy vision I throw a kick intended for his balls, and it lands on his kneecap instead.

He lets out a yelp. I blink several times but can't clear my vision. Marco reaches over, grabs my throat, and starts choking me.

Panic festers at the realization that I can't catch a breath. I cough. He squeezes tighter.

I focus on his blurry image, concentrate on cramming my fingers into his eye sockets, and hope to holy hell I'm hurting him. He screams and immediately releases his grip.

I gasp for air and ram my heel into his groin, this time hitting the mark. He grunts and cups his balls and falls to the carpet like the creepy little rat he is. I disengage the Taser cartridge, load another one, and, at close range, shoot.

Barbs sink into his chest, and he spasms into a twitching mess. Beneath my mask I let out a conquering laugh. *Take that, you asshole!* God, I want nothing more than to squeeze the trigger again, but I hold myself back. I have too many wonderful things in store.

I swallow, my throat tender, and concentrate on regaining my equilibrium. Pulling the zip ties from my side cargo pocket, I approach him. He tries to crawl away and I stalk him, loving the power it gives me over him. I can tell the .3 joules is starting to wear off, and so I roll him onto his stomach. He moans and makes a feeble attempt to get away, but I secure his wrists and ankles, then prop him up against the wall.

He spits right in my face.

Nasty. I punch him in the eye, glad his spit is on my mask and not my cheek.

I shove a handkerchief into his mouth and step away. I tune in to myself and realize I'm panting. The asshole wore me out. I take a second to center myself and blink my eyes a few times to clear the last remnants of whatever he sprayed in them. I hadn't expected him to be so challenging. But . . . I like it. The whole fight-and-chase thing adds an interesting element to the process. It elevates things to a more satisfying blood-pounding level.

I slip my hand into my back pocket and get out the reference list I'd printed.

It's repulsive and long, and although he served time, I can't believe he's not still in jail for what he did to those helpless animals.

Squatting down in front of him, I hold the list out and wait for him to read it, to recognize it.

His dark eyes slowly grow large as realization dawns. I'm here to do to him what he did to these animals.

He grunts and struggles against the zip ties, and I get to my feet.

From my cargo pants I pull out the supplies: a knife, a lighter, pliers, tacks, and a cigarette.

I lay them all in a neat line so he can see them, then I retrieve the BB gun from where he left it in the living room.

On the wall above his head I tack the printed list. I don't intend on doing all forty-six items, just the first five. Enough to show him the pain he's put vulnerable beings through.

1. Burned a cat seven times with a cigarette.

I take the cigarette and make a show of lighting it right in front of his face. I want him good and scared. I lower it toward his forearm, and he lets out a scream muffled by the handkerchief. I haven't even burned him yet. And to think I have seven of these to do. This isn't going to work.

I flip on his stereo and crank the volume, then pull a small roll of duct tape from my lower cargo pocket. As Victor says, duct tape has a million uses. How right he is. I peel off a strip and slap it over Marco's already-stuffed mouth.

Duct tape use number one million and one: to silence someone.

I take the cigarette and proceed. . . .

2. Pressed four tacks into a newborn kitten.
3. Used pliers to pull two toenails from a one-year-old puppy.
4. Shot an elderly blind dog ten times with a BB gun.
5. Carved an X into a poodle.

Each of his muted cries zings through my veins and tingles my capillaries. I ignore his whimpers and muffled pleas as I complete all five items. I feel nothing toward his pain but spirit and justice.

Slim justice.

I walk right out of his apartment, leaving him bloody, shaking with fear, and defenseless. Just like he left all forty-six of the animals he tortured.

I hope he's learned his lesson.

Chapter Twenty-Four

I GET HOME A LITTLE BEFORE MIDNIGHT to find Mom sitting on my bed. She's looking at my journal full of newspaper clippings, magazine articles, and printed pages on serial killers throughout time.

The Decapitator is on the last two pages, including the pieced-together picture he personally sent me.

I take a panicked step into my room. She looks up at me and gives my whole body a once-over. I fight the urge to check if Marco's blood is somewhere on me.

"Where have you been?" she asks.

I put my book bag down. "The usual." Studying at the coffeehouse.

She nods to my closet doors standing open and the shoe

box she found the journal in. "I was looking for stuff to donate to Goodwill."

I nod. She doesn't have to explain. I know she wasn't intentionally being nosy. It's not her style.

Mom holds up the journal. "How long have you had this?"

"Years," I honestly tell her.

"Why?"

"Serial killers intrigue me. Like . . . they intrigue you, I guess." This point must hit home, because she nods her understanding.

I watch as she flips through the book. I'm relieved I never jotted personal thoughts in it. That would really freak her out. Maybe in the back of my mind I knew something like this might happen someday.

She glances up at me. "Is there anything you want to tell me? Talk to me about?"

Where do I start? But I shake my head instead.

"You know if you ever want to talk to someone about your thoughts, you only need to tell me and I'll arrange it."

I move over to sit at my desk. "You mean like a psychiatrist?" Or a hypnotist.

Mom nods.

"I'm fine," I reassure her, hating that I've worried her. "Really." I motion to the book. "They fascinate me. That's it."

She flips to the back two pages and points to the picture the Decapitator sent me. "Where did you get this?"

"Decapitator fan site," I lie, although there are some out there. I've been to a couple. I'm sure Mom's FBI team has too.

It's a likely explanation. The head, arm, and leg individually were all over the Internet. That's what happens when a killer publicly reveals body parts. Any person with photo software can make it into a pieced-together photo.

Mom closes the book and leaves it on my bed as she gets up. "Thank you for your honesty. Goodnight, Lane."

She clicks my door shut behind her, and I immediately survey my clothes. No Marco blood. Good.

I sit down at my desk for a minute, staring at my journal. I've never come right out and asked my mom if something horrible happened to me when I was a kid. Sure, I asked her if I fell and hit my head, but that's it. I haven't really pursued the topic beyond that. Mainly because I think it would creep my mom out even more. She'd want to know why I want to know. She'd insist on professional help. She'd constantly be checking in.

No, I don't want nor do I need that intense attention.

I open up my journal and flip through it. I am my mother's daughter. Her fascination is my fascination. But when did it become so intense for her that it developed into her life's work?

This is the exact question I ask her the next morning.

In response, she gives me a long look, and just when I think she's not going to answer my question, she speaks. "When I was a little girl, my best friend lived next door. She was kidnapped, brutally murdered, and left in a ditch along the highway. Her killer was never caught. That single event changed the direction of my life."

I take a second to digest that, circling back around to the term "single event."

Mom puts the lid on her travel mug. "What about you, Lane? What's got you interested?"

I give an honest shrug. "I don't know."

"Maybe it's me," she offers.

"What do you mean?"

"I bring too much work home. I'm not as careful as I should be on the phone. I leave files in my office. . . ." She lets out a weary sigh, and I get the impression she's been thinking about this all night. Like she's the reason I have a warped mind.

I step forward and give her a hug. "You're a great mom." The best. "Please don't doubt that."

"I'm sorry," she whispers.

"Mom." I pull her in tighter. "You've done nothing wrong. You're careful around the house. If anything you're *overly* conscientious of keeping work and family separate."

If anything she could be a little freer with information, but of course I don't say that.

She nods and pulls away, and I can tell what I've said has made no difference in the way she feels.

What's funny is that I really don't care about making people feel better or okay about themselves. With Mom, though, it matters. I don't want her doubting herself. She really is about as good as parents come.

Justin barrels down the stairs. "Mom, you're coming today. Remember?"

She kisses the top of his head. "No *way* I'd miss your play."

"Dad, too?"

Mom nods. "He's meeting us at the school." She grabs her stuff and, without a glance in my direction, heads out the door.

I really could've used a last glance from her. Or even a *Bye, see you later, Lane.*

Justin looks up at me. "Daisy will *not* come out of the bathroom."

I'm not dealing with this right now. "Go use Mom and Dad's."

"All right, but if they yell at me later, you better tell them you gave me permission."

"I'll tell them."

Later, in first period, I'm sitting in my usual spot in the library, researching hypnosis. There's a whole site dedicated to the most popular programs used by psychiatrists in the treatment of patients with repressed memories. If there's something in me, maybe this time it'll come out. I find a reputable one by a

Dr. Jim Orland, pay for it, and download the MP3 file. I'll give it a try tonight.

From across the library Zach walks right toward me. "I heard about Belinda fighting you in the parking lot."

I get a little amused at how rumors morph. "We didn't fight."

"I'm sorry, Lane. I'm really sorry."

I like the way he always calls me Lane and not Slim. "I'm a big girl. I can take care of myself. So what if your ex has it in for me?"

Zach levels me with a long look. "Does anything scare you?"

"Rats kind of freak me out."

His mouth cocks up on one corner. "Why do you have to be so hot?"

"It's a gift." I crack a rare joke, and he laughs.

"Well, if you're not scared of Belinda and you ever want to no-strings-attached continue what we started over there"—he nods toward the bookshelf where my orgasm occurred—"then let me know."

I cock my mouth at the corner too. "I will."

With that he's gone, the bell rings, and I head to second period. By the end of the day Marco Morales is all the school can talk about.

"Whoever did it left the door cracked, and the neighbor

found him." This comment comes from the guy who sits behind me. "She called the cops, and Marco totally got busted for a ton of pot all over his apartment."

Good, the pot means he'll be back in jail.

"I bet it was the Masked Savior." This comes from the girl on my right. "Left a note nailed above his head and everything."

I'd *tacked* the note, but whatever. And . . . can we not find a better name than Masked Savior? It rings of a comic-book hero. Or in this case, heroine.

Last bell rings and I head home. Daisy's out with friends, my parents are at Justin's play, and I've got the whole house to myself. Time for a little Dr. Jim and self-hypnosis.

Knowing my iPod is in Daisy's room, I go straight there. As I open the door, jasmine incense hits me first. Then I glance over to see my sister going down on her new guy, West. I thought she said she was out with friends?

His back is to me, so he doesn't see me standing in the doorway. Daisy glances up and doesn't miss a beat. This isn't the first time I've seen her in action, and surely it won't be the last.

I walk over to her desk, where the incense is burning, grab my iPod, and head back out. West doesn't have a clue.

I speculate on Daisy's reasons behind giving so much head. I suspect she doesn't want an STD or to turn up pregnant. But does she realize she can get an STD in her mouth? Does she realize how nasty it is to be swallowing all that spunk?

Then again, maybe she spits.

Then again, maybe she needs to be paying more attention in health class.

Then again, perhaps she should perfect her hand job. Frankly, it's cleaner.

But my real question: What's up with the incense? She probably thinks it creates some sort of romantic environment.

As I shake my head at my own silly thought, I think of the time I accidentally walked in on my mom and stepdad. It was years ago and they never knew I saw. They were both naked on the floor in their bedroom. Victor was going down on my mom, and she had nipple clamps on. I exited, of course, just as fast as I had accidentally entered, but that image is forever singed in my brain. Nipple clamps—who knew my parents were so kinky.

My phone rings. "Hey, Reg."

"Yo. I'm going to send you a link to a blog I stumbled across earlier today."

"Blog?" I open my laptop and bring up my e-mail. "Blog about what?"

"The Decapitator."

I go really still. "Reg, I said I don't want you to do anything else with that. Please."

"I didn't. I programmed a Google search and forgot all about it. This landed in my spam."

I go to my inbox and follow the link to read:

Dear Decapitator: Still out there? Where's the other arm and leg?

Interesting. Seems I'm not the only one with that question on the brain. I scroll through the hundred or so comments and read a few:

[G_man] Dredge the Potomac.

[RocksTwinkies] You can decapitate me anytime.

[Alive@80] This is a gross blog!

One toward the end catches my attention:

[decap_itator] The next arm will be revealed to someone very special.

I read that again and know deep down that someone special is probably me.

Chapter Twenty-Five

THAT NIGHT I GO TO SLEEP LISTENING TO Dr. Jim's hypnosis track. I rarely dream and cannot recall ever having a nightmare, but an intense one occurs.

Blood.

Screams.

Stabbing.

I wake in a cold sweat.

"Lane?" Victor's standing over me. "You okay?" He leans down and feels my damp forehead. "You're burning up."

Disoriented, I sit up in bed and glance at my alarm clock. I overslept by an hour. I've never done that before.

"You're staying home," he decides. "I'll drop Justin and Daisy off and tell the school you're excused for the day."

I swallow and nod.

He rakes his concerned gaze over my sweaty hair and T-shirt stuck to my body. "Honey, do you need to go to the doctor?"

I shake my head, regaining some equilibrium. "I don't think so."

He gently pulls me out of bed. "I want you to get a shower, and I'm going to change your sheets. If you're not feeling better by noon, call me. Promise?"

I nod, shuffle off toward the bathroom, and take a very long cool bath. I've always been a shower taker. In fact, the last time I took a bath I think I was probably six or something.

When I return, he's changed my bed and left me buttered toast and orange juice on my desk. Slowly I sit down.

Blood. Screams. Stabbing.

What the hell did I remember?

An hour later I'm wandering around our house racking my brain back through the years and at the same time trying to forget whatever it is I remembered. At this point I'm not sure I *want* to remember.

Just as I'm thinking of going to school, I get a text from Zach. U OK?

YES. HOME "SICK."

LOL. U DON'T SOUND "SICK."

BORED, I type.

WANT SOME COMPANY?

I pause, considering. . . . If anything, it'll take my mind off my nightmare. YES, I punch back.

BE THERE IN 30.

Sure enough, thirty minutes later Zach rings my doorbell.

I open the door. "You make a habit out of skipping school?"

He steps over the threshold. "When the company's worth it."

I close the door. "We're alone."

"Exactly what I want to hear." Zach yanks me in for a thorough kiss. It's absolutely what I need. "You taste like butter."

"I had toast." And that's the last talking we do as we head straight up to my room.

My shirt goes first. Then my bra.

His shirt. Then his jeans.

My yoga pants. Then both our underwear.

This is messy. It's all I can think of as we have sex. But I roll with it. I do it. I get it over with and get in the shower as soon as I can.

When I get out, Zach's made sandwiches and is sitting on my rumpled bed in his underwear. I smile a little. "You didn't have to do that."

He shrugs. "Least I could do."

I slip on a T-shirt and clean undies and sit across from him.

He reaches for a sandwich. "Why didn't you tell me you were a virgin?"

"Why? Is it important?"

Zach shakes his head with a slight laugh—"Guess it's not"— and shoves a huge bite in his mouth.

I grab a PB&J and take a bite.

He chews and swallows, all the while studying me. "It'll be better the next time."

There's not going to be a next time. As far as I'm concerned, I've officially checked it off the list. However, I will do another orgasm in the library. Now *that* I enjoyed.

"You're . . . you're aggressive in bed."

No, what I do in bed, I discover, is forget about everything else. *Blood. Screams. Stabbing.*

I take a look at his thoughtful expression. "Did I scare you?" I like Zach. I don't want to scare him.

He winks. "Good scare."

That makes me smile.

"With Belinda I was always drunk. This is the first sober sex I've had in a long time." He reaches out and touches my knee. "Lane . . ."

If this is the point where we emotionally connect, I'd rather have sex again.

Zach puts his sandwich aside, climbs off the bed, and gets dressed. "I won't bore you with mushy talk. Don't worry."

I do love how he can read my mind.

He zips up his jeans. "We'll take it slower next time. More romantic."

I'm not sure how to tell him there's probably not going to be a next time.

Zach gives me a sweet kiss. "Later."

After he leaves, I lie back on my bed and close my eyes. I fantasize how that would've played out with Dr. Issa and get more excited from that than I did with Zach.

After my fantasy plays out, I call Reggie.

"Aren't you supposed to be in class?" she answers.

"I'm home sick, having sex."

Reggie coughs. "I'm sorry, did you say sex? *And?*"

"Eh."

Reggie laughs at that.

"I'm in love with West," Daisy announces that night at dinner.

"You sure get in love a lot," Justin points out, and Daisy shoots him a look.

I adore my little brother.

He turns those innocent hazel eyes on me. "How come you're never in love?"

Good question.

"Love?" Daisy snorts. "Lane doesn't feel *anything*."

"Daisy." Mom reprimands her.

My sister's right. I don't feel anything.

Well, that's not really true. Justin's smile tickles my insides. Dr. Issa's massages them. And when I stalk a perp, it's euphoric.

I do crave that charge that percolates through my cells.

"I saw Zach talking to that girl," Daisy informs me. "What's her name? Belinda?"

Daisy knows full well what her name is.

She cuts into her salmon. "They seemed real friendly."

"Well good for Zach and Belinda." Does Daisy think this really troubles me?

"Girls." It's Victor's turn to reprimand.

I don't bother pointing out I haven't done anything. He already knows it anyway. Parents are obligated to be impartial with warnings like "girls" or "boys." I realize this.

He stands. "I'm on a red-eye. See you all in a few days."

"Dad?" Justin stops him.

"Yeah?"

"What all states have you been to?"

He thinks about that a second. "Oregon, Arizona, Tennessee, Minnesota, Maine, Wyoming . . ." He continues listing states. "Why do you ask?"

"Social studies project. Suppose you can help me with it when you get back?"

He musses Justin's hair. "Sure."

As he goes to get his suitcase, I rewind what he's just said. Oregon, Arizona, Tennessee, Minnesota, Maine, Wyoming . . .

With kisses to everyone, he heads toward the door. "Lane,

you had some mail today. I put it all on your desk. Looked like college stuff."

"Thanks." Or maybe the Decapitator has contacted me again.

After Victor leaves, Mom heads to her office, Daisy goes upstairs, and me and Justin clean up. Oregon, Arizona, Tennessee . . . I wonder if Victor was involved with investigating the other decapitations. For whatever reason, it hadn't occurred to me that he might have been. I mean, I know he and Mom work for the same division, but Mom's always the one bringing home serial-killer work, not Victor. Actually, I can't recall Victor ever bringing home any work. And the times I've asked him about his work, he always says the same thing: "Sweetheart, you know much of what I do is top secret. I'm sorry."

He may very well know just as much about the Decapitator as my mom. Maybe more if he's been investigating all along.

"*SpongeBob's* on," Justin informs me and parks it in front of the TV. I don't know why he likes that show. I've watched it a few times, and it's kind of stupid. But whatever amuses my little brother, I guess.

I head to my room where the stack of mail waits and start opening it. Mostly college-app junk just like Victor thought. Fact is, I've got my sights on UVA. I could care less about all the other ones. I haven't been accepted yet, but I have absolutely no reason to doubt I will be. Victor's an alumnus, and my scores more than exceed qualifying levels.

A large white envelope is at the bottom of the stack. The return address is:

POOLE AND TRIPPE, ATTORNEYS AT LAW
WASHINGTON, DC

Inside is a bunch of paperwork. I shovel through it, trying to make sense. There's a death certificate for Seth Leaf, my real father, dated one week ago. Wait a minute. *One week ago?* And a deed to 4 Buchold Place in my name. *My name?*

I grab the whole thing up and go to find Mom. *What* is going on?

Chapter Twenty-Six

A FEW MINUTES LATER I KNOCK ON MY
mom's office door.

"Yes?" she calls. "Just a sec." I hear a rustling of papers.
"Okay, come in."

I hand her the big white envelope with the death certificate
right on top and wait to see how she's going to explain this one.

She takes her time flipping through the papers. "Close the
door," she finally says.

I do and take a seat beside her desk.

Mom looks right at me. "Clearly, I've lied to you."

Not what I expected her to say, but okay.

"Seth Leaf, your real father, has known about you your
entire life. I'm going to be brutally honest. He never wanted a

thing to do with you. When I met and married your stepdad, Seth agreed to sign off all rights to you. Your stepdad and I decided to tell you Seth was dead to save you from emotional distress."

I take a second to digest all this. "Where has Seth been all this time?"

Mom shrugs. "I don't communicate with him. I do know he's been in and out of mental institutions for years."

"*Mental* institutions?"

Mom sits back in her chair. "Do you remember I told you his dad died?"

I nod.

"Seth killed him."

What?

Mom's expression gentles. "Your grandfather was not a nice man. He horribly beat your grandmother and both the boys."

"I thought you said my grandfather was a pastor. Wait— *both* the boys?"

"Your grandfather *was* a pastor. And Seth has a younger brother."

"I have an uncle?"

Mom nods. "He's younger than Seth by three years. Anyway, your grandfather was beating your uncle and Seth defended him. Your grandfather ended up dying."

"And grandmother?"

"She committed suicide not long after."

"And my uncle?"

Mom sighs. "Like Seth. In and out of mental institutions his whole life."

"So he's still alive?"

"As far as I know."

Oh my God. Seventeen years. For seventeen years I thought my real father was from a loving Christian home. I thought he grew up as this special boy, served his country as a decorated marine, mourned the loss of his parents, and died a tragic, unexpected death.

Everything I spent my whole life believing was a big effing lie. I don't have some dark memory that I need hypnosis to unravel. It's in my blood. An abusive grandfather, a suicidal grandmother, a father and uncle who have been in and out of mental institutions. No wonder I am the way I am. I shove all ten fingers into my hair and drop my head into my hands. I have nothing but hate and violence running in my veins.

"You remind me a lot of Seth," Mom softly admits as she has before.

Funny, I don't take that as a compliment.

"Stoic," she clarifies. "He rarely showed emotions." She leans forward and puts her hand on my knee. "Do you understand why I didn't tell you about all this?"

I brush her hand away. "No, I don't."

She doesn't move, and I get the impression she's trying extremely hard to figure out what to say or do next.

"Would you have told me eventually?"

"Yes. Your stepdad and I both knew the time would come. We just didn't realize it would be tonight."

What were you waiting on? I want to immediately snap. *For me to mature? Because I've been mature for a very long time now.*

"How do you feel?" Mom cautiously asks.

I've always hated that question. How do I *feel*? Angry at being kept in the dark and finally, *finally* hearing some significant facts. Facts I could've handled years ago instead of spending so much time wondering about myself.

"Are you okay?" she tries again.

"No, I'm not okay. It's probably going to be a long time before I am. My whole other side of the family is a giant lie. Why would you think I'm okay?"

She doesn't have an answer for that.

"What about Four Buchold Place?"

She frowns. "Where?"

I pull the deed from the paperwork.

Mom looks it over. "Herndon . . . this is the place his brother lived."

"So you've been there?"

"Yes. Only one time. Even back then it was broken down. I can only imagine what it looks like now."

"I need to go there. Will you go with me?"

"Of course."

Now? But I know that's not reasonable. "Tomorrow?"

Mom picks up the big white envelope. "Tell you what, I'll call this law firm and get more information."

"Okay."

She turns to her computer. "I'm sorry to do this to you, but—"

"No," I interrupt. "Don't start working. Now is not the time. Can't you see I'm upset?"

Cautiously Mom takes in my expression. "Lane . . ."

"Mom, you lied to me. It's going to take more than 'save me from emotional distress' to explain this to me. You should've told me about this years ago."

"I know." She sighs. "I'm sorry. You'll understand one day when you're a parent."

"I hate when adults say that!"

Her phone rings. She glances at it and then guiltily up to me. "I've got a ton of work to do. Can we talk more later?"

"Fine," I grit out through clenched teeth. Although I know there won't be a later. There's really nothing more to be said. I trudge upstairs to my room and slam my door.

If my real dad just died, then he definitely *could've* been the one messing with me this whole time. It all makes sense now. The letters. My own dark urges. The weird fascination and connection to killers.

No wonder I'm messed up. My real father could have very well been the Decapitator, which still aggravatingly does not explain James Donner coming forward.

The next day at school all I can think about is 4 Buchold Place, my real dad, details of the decapitations, and what James Donner has to do with all this.

And the more time I spend thinking the more something just seems off. Untied. Loose. Disconnected. Or maybe I'm telling myself that so I don't have to deal with the fact my real dad might have been a serial killer.

I don't know. It's all frustrating, depressing, and not nearly as tied up and connected as it should be. As far as 4 Buchold, I definitely want to see inside.

I've thought about Mom a lot today as well, and . . . I understand why she kept everything from me. She was trying to protect me. I don't agree with it, and am definitely still angry with her, but I get it.

By last period it occurs to me I haven't seen Zach all day. Even if it's just across the room, we at least see each other at lunch. And to think just yesterday he and I—

"Did you get a load of Zach's lip?" my lab partner asks.

He and Zach play soccer. He knows Zach and I have hung out. "No. What's wrong with his lip?"

My lab partner shrugs. "Dunno. He's got stitches."

Stitches? He'd been kissing me with those lips just yesterday. He said I tasted like butter.

I never look for people after school. Today, though, I look for Zach. I see him at his locker, and he sees me—I know he does—but he acts like he doesn't. Normally I could care less if people avoid me, but it matters this time.

He ducks into the bathroom, I'm sure convinced when he emerges I'll be gone, but I'm not. I'm standing right at the entrance when he comes out.

He takes one look at me, and it's more than obvious he doesn't want me seeing him.

I check out the row of stitches bisecting his bottom lip. "Gonna tell me what happened?"

"I fell. Listen—"

"Fell off what?"

"The . . . stairs at our house. Actually the outside stairs." He looks around. "I've got to go." With that he heads off down the hall.

I let him, but I know he didn't fall. Of course he didn't. That lip looks like someone hit him.

My cell buzzes and I check the display. It's from Reggie. CALL ME. IT'S ABOUT YOUR DAD.

I ALREADY KNOW, I type back. This has got to go down in history as the first time I know something before her.

EVERYTHING? she texts back.

169

I dial her number. Sometimes there's too much to say for texting.

"Institutionalized," she answers. "Killed his father. Mother committed suicide. Younger brother currently missing."

"Yes to all. But . . . brother currently missing?"

"No known address. Hasn't been officially seen in years. Could be living in a ditch of some third-world country for all anyone knows."

Or could be decapitating people. Hell, for all I know my real dad and my uncle were partners in all this mess.

"Thanks," I tell her. "Mom and I are going to Four Buchold Place when I get home. I'll let you know how it goes."

Daisy's waiting at the Jeep when I get to the parking lot. "Like what you saw the other day? West reciprocated, by the way."

I don't bother telling her to shut up. What a slut.

We get Justin from school, and he launches into the longest story in history about finding a dead mouse on the playground. Even Daisy gets bored, and she's pretty good about the giving-our-little-brother-patience thing.

Mom's already home when we get there. "Daisy, watch Justin. Lane and I have someplace to go."

"Well, it's a good thing I don't have plans," Daisy snarks back.

Mom ignores her.

"How are you doing today?" Mom asks a few minutes into the trip.

"Fine." Really, what kind of question is "How are you doing"? How does she think I'm doing—Jesus!

She takes the cue I'm not in the mood to talk, and flips on her GPS, and we get onto the toll road to Herndon.

"Yes, this looks vaguely familiar," she comments some thirty minutes later as she pulls onto Buchold Place.

She watches the numbers on the houses while I look straight ahead at our destination. Number four looks different in the daylight. Not so deserted. Like someone may have been here since I came last.

Mom pulls onto the side driveway. She kills the engine and slips a key from her purse. "Picked this up from the law firm today."

I take it from her outstretched hand, and we both get out of the car.

"Doesn't look as shabby as I thought it would after all these years." She gives it a second look. "No, I'm wrong. It's pretty shabby."

I make my way under the huge oak tree in the front yard and across the brick walkway littered with weeds.

We step up onto the porch and it creaks.

One huge spiderweb spans the corner of the porch, and a swing sits half on, half off its chain.

I fit the key into the old lock, click it open, and, feeling more curious than anything, step inside.

Mustiness hits me. But it's not too bad. Maybe a few weeks' worth of mustiness in lieu of months or years.

I turn to the right, where a well-worn brown plaid couch sits. To the left is a window, broken and boarded up. I cross through the room and into a small kitchen with yellow lino-leum, an old refrigerator, and no stove.

Mom opens the refrigerator to reveal one lone box of bak-ing soda.

I test the light switch and find the electricity on. Someone's been living here. Most likely my real father.

Above the sink sits a window that looks out over a back-yard full of leaves with a rusted swing set off to the left.

A child's laughter echoes in my ears, and I glance around the yard but see only the wet leaves and empty swings. "Have I been here before?"

"No. Not that I know of," replies Mom.

I turn to her. "Not that you *know* of?"

She sighs, and that sigh tells me there's yet another story to tell.

"When you were three," she begins, "Seth . . . took you. You were only gone for the afternoon, and he brought you back, guilty, apologizing. By then the police had gotten involved, but I decided not to file charges. The next day Seth signed away rights to you. And he's never seen you again."

I slump back against the sink. "Why didn't you tell me this last night?"

Mom sighs again. "I don't know, Lane. But I promise you that's the last bit of information I kept from you. I promise."

Unbelievable. Another lie. I'm so pissed, I can't do anything but just stare darts at her.

She closes her eyes in—I don't know—guilt, frustration. "Lane, please don't hate me."

Logically I realize this is stressful for her, dredging up a past she thought long gone. But this is stressful for me, too. Surely she gets that. I push past her. "Let's just see the rest and get out of here." I step through the other side of the kitchen and down a wood-planked hall.

"From what I remember there's only one bedroom and one bathroom." She points to a white door. "That's the bathroom."

It already sits open a few inches, and I push it the rest of the way. A chipped claw-footed tub with no curtain crowds the small space. Beside it sits a toilet with no lid and a sink with old-fashioned hot and cold knobs. I twist the cold and water runs out.

"Do you suppose Seth has been living here? The water's on, the electricity's on, and although the place is run-down, it's obviously been kept up by somebody."

Mom nods. "You read my mind. It does seem to have had

some life in it." She motions to the bedroom. "Let's see the last room."

I take the few steps past her, reach out, and turn the porcelain knob. The door creaks open.

Screams shatter the walls.

Blood sprays the ceiling.

Sun glints off a long knife.

I stumble back.

Mom grabs me. "Lane?"

I shut my eyes. A blond woman, eyes wide with fear, reaches out. *Help me.*

"Lane?" Mom shakes me.

I turn and race from the house.

Chapter Twenty-Seven

I'M SILENT THE WHOLE WAY HOME. I DON'T know what I remembered, but something happened in that house, in that bedroom, and I was there to witness it.

I go straight to my room, ignoring Mom's worried looks, and close my door.

I don't go down to dinner, and at nine o'clock Mom brings me a bowl of tomato soup. "Want to talk?"

"No." I take the soup and note my hands are still shaking.

Mom glances down at my garbage can. "Lane, did you throw up?"

"Yes."

"Are you sick?" She feels my head.

"No." Whatever happened to me in that house scared the

living shit out of me. "I don't ever want to go back to Four Buchold Place again." I don't care that the Decapitator has ties there. I'm done.

She nods. "Okay. You don't have to."

"Thank you."

"I found out your uncle owned it first and then sold it to your father. That's how it ended up getting willed to you."

Maybe Seth should've willed it back to my uncle. Because I don't want it.

"I also found out how Seth died."

Murder? Decapitation? Or something equally sinister I'm sure.

"Colon cancer."

"Oh." This strikes me as odd. Such a normal way to die.

"I'll arrange to get it sold. We'll put the money in your college account. Sound good?"

Sounds *more* than good.

Concern gentles her already troubled expression. "I've never seen you like that before. It worries me."

It worries me, too.

"Don't feel like you have to do your Saturday shift at Patch and Paw."

"I want to." Corn Chip will be there this weekend, and I definitely want to see him.

Mom gives me a long look. "I don't know what you remembered, but please, *please* feel free to talk to me. Okay?"

"Okay." Absolutely not.

"Are you stilled pissed with me?"

"Honestly, I've done nothing but relive Four Buchold. I haven't had time to think about you. But now that you ask. Yes, I'm still pissed."

"Fair enough. Do you want to talk?"

"No. I want to be left alone."

"I'll be in my office if you need anything." She grabs my garbage can and heads out.

I sit for a while, staring at the parmesan grated on top of the soup. Eventually I eat it, even though I'm only mildly hungry, and go to bed. I sleep like usual, like the dead, with no dreams.

I don't see my mom in the morning and wonder if she planned it that way. Maybe she really *doesn't* know how to deal with me and would rather ignore the whole thing.

Either way, by ten a.m. I'm playing with Corn Chip in Patch and Paw's side yard.

I throw the tennis ball. He goes after it and brings it back. Happy. Clueless.

I give his scraggly gray ear a rub right where I know he likes it best. He leans in to the rub, proving he does, indeed, prefer it there the most.

"I don't know what I'm going to do," I tell him. "My life is a little too weird right now."

Flashbacks. Messages from a serial killer. Lies.

"Tell me about it," Dr. Issa comments.

I glance over my shoulder to see him standing behind me. He has a way of sneaking up on me. I don't care for it at all.

Quietly he approaches. "Do you know what's going on with Zach?"

"What do you mean?"

Dr. Issa tucks his hands in his lab coat. "Have you seen his lip?"

I nod. "He said he fell."

"Did he, now?"

"Down some stairs," I provide.

"There are no stairs in our father's condo."

"He said outside."

Dr. Issa shakes his head. "There're no stairs outside *or* in."

I wait. I really don't know what he wants me to say. We both know Zach's lying.

"He's not telling the truth." Dr. Issa confirms my thoughts.

"I see."

Dr. Issa glances back to the building like he's making sure no one's listening. "I don't know how much Zach has shared with you, but . . . he's had a pretty hard couple of years. When our mom died, he really went over the edge. But he's been doing so well lately. Being your . . . *friend* has made him happy."

Friend. I catch the emphasis. "I'm glad."

He glances through the fenced side yard to my keyed Jeep in the parking lot. "Zach told me Belinda did that."

"She did."

"I'm 99.9 percent sure she busted Zach's lip."

Corn Chip nudges my hand and I give him a pet. "Why are you telling me this?"

"I want you to be careful. And I want you to watch out for Zach. He may seem okay, but he's still pretty fragile." Dr. Issa brings his brown eyes from the parking lot to mine. "I don't want him sliding back into his old life."

"Seems like Zach's fairly levelheaded."

"I don't want him sliding back into his old life," Dr. Issa repeats, this time with more emphasis.

I get it. I'll pay Belinda a visit later.

And that's exactly what I do after work. I park my Wrangler and walk right up to her door, just like she did to mine.

I ring the bell.

Her dad answers. "Yes?"

I flash him a bright, un-Lane-like smile. "Hi! I'm a friend of Belinda's. Is she home?"

Her dad smiles back. "Yes. Belinda!" he shouts.

A couple seconds later she steps into view.

"Hi, Belinda!" I channel the cheerleader not in me. "I'm going to the mall! Want to come?"

She narrows her eyes and I innocently blink.

"That sounds like fun," her dad encourages. "You don't have any plans, Belinda. Go on."

Thanks, Dad. Now she doesn't have an excuse.

I blink again, maintaining my smile, knowing she can't get out of this.

She plasters on a grin matching my own. "Sure. Let me just get my purse."

"I'll drive!" I volunteer.

As we climb into my Wrangler, her dad waves from the door. "Be back by eleven!"

He closes the door and both our grins fall away.

"What do you want?" she spits. *"Bitch!"*

No, I'm having none of that. I elbow her in the throat, and while she gags, I slowly pull away. I'm fully aware I'm driving and this isn't the smartest of moves. I'm fully aware I'm filled with rage that has just a little bit to do with her and everything to do with the built-up stress and tension over Seth, the Decapitator, and my mom's lies. Yes, I'm fully aware of these things and really don't care.

"Here's the thing," I start. "I don't much care for people who mess with me or my friends."

She makes a grab for me and I dodge it, swerving in my lane, overcorrecting, and then following up with a pop to her nose. "That'll stop bleeding in a little bit." I shift into second, open my glove compartment, and hand her a couple of McDonald's napkins. "Word of warning. Don't leave a mess in my Jeep."

She presses the napkins to her nose and shoots me a glare. "You're insane."

Oh, Belinda, you have no idea. "So here's what you're going to do. You're going to cough up the money to get my Jeep fixed and you're going to leave Zach alone."

She makes another grab for me, succeeds in yanking my hair, and then lets out an evil giggle.

I shove her head into the dash. "Oh, look; you fell."

Belinda scowls at me through teary eyes.

"Mess with me anytime. I'm always up to the challenge."

Someone honks at me, and I realize I'm hovering over the white line. I slow down and pull off to the side of the road.

"What do you want?" she sobs.

"Little slow, are we? I already told you. Fix my Jeep and leave Zach alone."

"Take me home," she whines.

"Why? I'm just getting started."

Her eyes widen in fear, and *that's* the exact look I've been waiting for.

She goes for me again, like the stupid girl she is. I grab her knee and work my thumb beneath her patella.

"Okay!" she screams. "Let me go!"

I press a little further just to make a point and, well, to hear her scream again. "Do we have an understanding?"

Through tears, she nods.

"Say it," I command.

"Fix your Jeep. Leave Zach alone."

I put my Jeep in gear, circle her block, and let her out at a 7-Eleven. "Get yourself cleaned up and walk home. I'll send you the bill for the Jeep."

She opens the door and stumbles out. "I hate you."

"Good." I reach over, close her door, and drive off.

Oh my God, how exhilarating. How unbelievably adrenaline charged . . .

My cell buzzes and snaps me back. I check the text display.

GREAT JOB. LOVED WHAT U DID TO THE GIRL.

My gaze jumps to the rearview mirror right as my cell buzzes again. DON'T WORRY. I'M LONG GONE BY NOW.

Again I pull over to the side of the road. WHO IS THIS?

JAMES DONNER IS NOT THE DECAPITATOR.

& U'RE NOT MY REAL FATHER. HE CAN'T BE TEXTING ME FROM THE GRAVE.

AH, CATCHING ON R U?

I wait to see what he'll type next.

JAMES DONNER IS NOT THE DECAP, he repeats.

PROVE IT, I type back.

MEET ME @ 4 BUCHOLD PLACE & I WILL.

My hearts leaps to light speed as I read and reread the last text. *4 Buchold Place?* No . . .

CHOOSE NOT TO SHOW & I WILL HUNT U. I WILL HURT U. I WILL MAKE YOUR FAMILY SUFFER.

I close my eyes and spend a good solid minute just breathing, just calming my rapid-fire pulse. *I will hunt you.*

Why? Why me? He wants to meet me or give me something or, hell, I don't know. If this is the only way, then I have to do it. I have to go. I have to find out who the Decapitator is and how this is all connected to me.

I will make your family suffer.

I think of the picture he took of me coming out of school. And of the one he snapped of Daisy. An image of my little brother flashes into my mind and shoots a searing pain right into my heart. *Justin* . . .

I grab my phone and with a shaky hand type back, OK WHEN?

Chapter Twenty-Eight

AS USUAL I'M UP BEFORE EVERYBODY ELSE on Sunday morning. I'm sitting at our dining room table on my laptop, sipping my dark brew when I get a text.

R U UP? It's from Zach.

YES.

My phone rings and I answer it. "And here I thought I was the only one who gets up this early on Sunday morning."

"I haven't really gone to sleep," Zach says.

Neither had I after the Decapitator's contact.

"Belinda came to my house last night," he continues.

Of course she did. The helpless female that she is. "And?"

"Although she didn't come right out and say it, I got the distinct impression you're the person who assaulted her."

Assaulted?

Yes, I guess I did beat the shit out of her. Rewind the clock and I could've handled things differently. Talked to her. Hit her once, not multiple times. I'm irritated with myself for allowing my temper such free reign. "And what about what she did to you?"

"That's none of your business, Lane."

"I see."

Neither one of us speaks for a while, and I begin to wonder if he's hung up.

"You're not . . . you're not the person I thought you were," he says finally, breaking the static silence.

"And what kind of person did you think I was?" I suppose now's as good a time as any for him to see I have a dark side too, just like Belinda.

He pauses. "Unique. Intelligent. Quiet. Focused. Dry humor, even though you don't show it to a lot of people."

Hm. I've never heard anyone describe me before. It's not half-bad.

"But not this," he finishes. "I never took you for violent."

Violent. I'm not quite sure that's the term I would've used. Deranged, maybe, but in an okay way—if that's even possible.

"I don't think we can be friends anymore," he finishes.

Normally this type of thing doesn't faze me, but an emptiness pangs inside me at his words. It occurs to me I should probably try to argue the point. . . .

"Don't worry," he goes on. "She's not going to tell her parents. This will remain between the three of us."

I *wasn't* worried. It doesn't matter anyway. Belinda never intended on telling her parents. This has always been about Zach, his pity, and winning him back. Belinda should get an Oscar for this.

"Say something?" he encourages.

"Why?" He just said he doesn't want to be friends.

Zach sighs. "Good-bye, Lane." He clicks off.

I sit for a second, thinking it all through. In my own twisted way I really thought I was doing the right thing. In hindsight I should've seen this coming. Of course she'd go straight to Zach and play on his emotions. What better ammunition against me? What better way to get him back?

This is ultimately what I wanted, though. To cut ties with Zach, with the drama. I never have done nor will I ever do drama. I'm a very black-and-white person. It's either this way or that.

And that's exactly how I prefer it. In my opinion it's the only way a person can effectively function.

Yes, I convince myself of all this and refuse to acknowledge the empty pang that hearing *I don't think we can be friends anymore* brought on.

I log on to my laptop and compose a news search on 4 Buchold Place. I concentrate on fourteen years ago. I would've been three the year Seth took me on that one afternoon. I dig around, doing my limited cyber-searching, coming up with of course nothing, and wish more than anything I had Reggie's skills.

CALL ME WHEN U'RE UP, I text her, and continue digging through cyberlinks.

Three hours later my family's getting up. Mom starts making breakfast, Victor and Justin read the funnies, and Daisy's in the bathroom.

The all-American family.

Reggie calls. "Yes?"

"Okay, I'm going to information dump on you." I tell her about the lies Mom has told, about the freaked-out memory I had while visiting 4 Buchold, and about being kidnapped by Seth when I was three.

"Whoa," she mumbles.

"Reg, I need to know what happened in that house fourteen years ago. Can you help me? Can you shovel your way through whatever firewall there is and get the information? Police reports, FBI . . . I don't know. But I need help. Something significant happened, and no one's telling me what it is."

"Okay. I'll do what I can. Give me till noon?"

I blow out a relieved breath. "Thank you. Yes, noon is fine."

I sit through breakfast with my family, but with Zach, the Decapitator, Reggie, Seth, Mom's lies, and about a ton of other things it's all I can do to halfway seem normal over bacon, eggs, and pancakes. It's too bad, because bacon ranks fairly high on my favorite-food list.

By noon I'm incessantly checking my messages.

At one Reggie finally calls me.

"Your attention to time is one of the things that annoys me the most," I bitch at her.

She totally ignores my sarcasm. "You're not going to believe what I found. I had to dig deep. Some files were locked."

I close my bedroom door. "Go on."

"You were most definitely there. God, Lane, I'm going to send you a picture, and I don't want you to freak."

I wake my laptop and pull up my e-mail. "I'm ready."

A few seconds later Reggie's name pops up with an attachment. I open it . . . and freeze.

"Yes, when you were three"—Reggie starts talking—"you disappeared from your house. With your mom and stepdad both being connected to the FBI, there was an all-out manhunt for you. You were found some eight hours later at Four Buchold Place. You were mute. Sitting on that blood-soaked bed. Holding the blond woman's hand. Staring into her dead eyes. She'd been stabbed twenty-nine times."

Silently I stare at the picture, at the red-haired toddler—me—covered in the woman's blood and clinging to her hand.

"They never found the killer," Reggie quietly goes on. "And

although you never spoke, they speculated you saw the whole thing."

I finally find my voice. "Wh-where did you get this picture?"

"I hacked into the FBI. According to the report your mom received an anonymous tip that that's where you'd been taken."

"Mom knew about all this and she didn't tell me?" She'd watched me freak in that bedroom and knew why. How *dare* she keep this from me.

"Your mom's trying to protect you." Reggie defends her.

"But she'd promised she told me everything. I believed her. How many more things is she keeping from me? It's like I don't even know her."

Reggie sighs. "Want my two cents?"

"No."

"Let it go. Don't be mad at your mom and stepdad. They love you. If you had a daughter that had been through something so horrible, you'd probably do the same thing."

No. I don't think I would.

It all starts trickling back. The years of them carefully watching me, explaining away my emotionless self by saying I was simply different and unique. The years of them encouraging me to embrace myself and walk to my own beat. The years of counseling we all went to just to make sure we were healthy and happy.

They'd simply been assisting me in repressing the nightmare, watching, waiting for signs of remembrance.

Likely, their FBI psych department counseled them to handle it that way.

"You still there?" Reggie asks.

"Did my real father stab that woman?" Who else—it's his house and he was the one who took me.

"No one has proof. To this day it is an unsolved crime."

"Well, was he at least brought in for questioning?"

"Yes, but according to the reports, he left you in the care of that woman, stepped out for a grocery run, came back, and found the scene."

The Decapitator's first documented kill had been thirteen years ago, one year after this murder. "What month was this picture taken?"

Reggie takes a second to look that up. "September."

The same month the Decapitator kills.

"I know you can't tell from the picture and all the blood, but whoever stabbed that woman tried to saw off her arms, legs, and head," Reggie tells me.

I get really still. This has got to be the Decapitator's first attempt. Surely the FBI's made this connection.

No wonder he's been contacting me, following me. The Decapitator's first attempt . . . and I was there to witness it.

Nature versus nurture: I never had a fighting chance. I've been ruined from both angles.

Chapter Twenty-Nine

FULLY AWARE I'M BREAKING CURFEW AND in no way caring, I park my Jeep down the street from 4 Buchold Place just a few minutes before midnight. Like the last time I was here this late, the street and its few houses sit shadowed, and aside from a car here or there, fairly empty.

In my left cargo pocket sits my Taser. In my right is the tranquilizer gun, already loaded and with the safety on. Zip ties lie in an untangled circle in my back right button flap. Duct tape takes up my calf pocket.

I desperately try to ignore my thumping heart as I go through the motions of wrapping my springy hair into a ponytail and cramming it up inside my ski mask. Preparations, I'm discovering, serve to not only build the anticipation but also provide focus for events about to transpire.

With one last glance around the dark street, I wedge my fingers into my black leather gloves, turn the dome light off in my Jeep, and quietly climb out.

I'm not sure what to expect, but I'm not taking any chances. I *will* use the tranquilizer if I have to. I will use *all* of it without a second thought. This much I'm sure of.

Staying in the shadows and under the enormous oak trees, I silently make my way to the dark house. I ignore my shallow breathing and my rapid pulse, and focus on what is about to happen. I'm either going to meet the Decapitator or he is going to reveal the next body part to me. I can't see that anything else is going to happen.

I crouch behind a bush and survey the area. Same wet leaves cover the ground as the other day. A slight October breeze rustles through the bushes and the branches of the trees. I catch a faint hint of chimney smoke lingering in the air. It's not cold enough for a fire.

Carefully I survey the house. Top to bottom. Left to right. And see no movement.

I wait for a sign. Does he want me to come in the front door?

"Stop right there!"

I freeze.

Mom?

"Don't move!" Her voice resonates from the backyard.

I leave the bush I'm crouched behind and make my way in that direction.

A shot goes off and I plaster myself to the side of the house. *Oh my God!* Was that aimed at me?

Up and down the street, a few lights flip on.

The sound of two people fighting echoes through the night. *Mom?*

"Stop!" my mom shouts, and then immediately sucks in air.

I peek around the corner to see her drop to the wet leaves holding her side. From the tree branch above her head dangles the missing arm.

In the moonlight blood glistens off her hand. Has she been shot?

She groans and I don't hesitate in racing toward her.

She sees me coming and tries to crawl away. I want to speak, I want to tell her it's going to be okay, but I know I can't. She'll recognize my voice. For that matter, she might recognize my body even if it is completely covered.

I come down beside her and reach for her bloody hand. So much blood.

She stops struggling, maybe realizing I'm here to help.

"I've been stabbed," she gasps.

She's wearing her Kevlar vest, but the knife went up under it.

What are you doing here? I want to scream.

Sirens pierce the air and I automatically jerk to attention. *I can't be here!*

She grabs my wrist, and in that second I understand she can't let me go. She doesn't know who I am, but she knows I have something to do with all this.

I twist from her strong grip and take off into the night.

The sirens get closer, and I know she'll have help soon.

I climb in my Wrangler and stealthily pull away.

Mom's been stabbed! I fight every urge in me to go back to her and instead concentrate on driving away. Help will come soon, I reassure myself.

Oh, God, what if he pierced an organ when he stabbed her? She could be dead right now in that backyard, and instead of waiting by her side, I ran.

She may have recognized me!

The Decapitator must have invited us both. He wanted us to meet. Or maybe he intended on getting me caught. What kind of sick game is he playing, stabbing my mother?

I park in the shadows of a nearby playground and watch as an ambulance and cops swarm the neighborhood.

The neighbors probably called when they heard the gunshot. Or maybe Mom's team was nearby. If the FBI was watching the neighborhood, they probably saw my Jeep pull in. They may have even seen me hiding in the shadows. They're all going to connect the dots now if they haven't already. The house. The Decapitator. Me. I don't know what I'm going to do.

Another siren blares past me and I jerk.

I close my eyes, smothered in guilt. I'm a horrible daughter. I can't lose my mom. *I can't.*

The ambulance peels out of the neighborhood, sirens blaring. Blaring sirens are a good thing. It means she's still alive. Right?

Mom's supposed to have backup, a partner at least. She shouldn't have gone in there by herself. What the hell was she thinking?

None of the cops leave the neighborhood, and I assume they're scouring every inch of the property. Roadblocks will go up soon. I've got to get out of here.

I stow my gear, change out of my clothes, and drive home. I want to go to the hospital but know I can't. If I do, they'll know I know. And they'll want to know *how* I know. I pray Victor is up, but he's not. Does he know yet? Surely they would've called him by now.

I lie awake the whole night, guilt eating me from every angle. I left my mom to protect my own identity. This is all my fault. I should've never kept any of this to myself. He threatened me, my family . . . I did what he said and he double-crossed me!

At five a.m. I'm up, waiting, waiting for someone to come tell me everything's okay.

At six a.m. Victor finds me standing in the kitchen. "You three kids aren't going to school today."

A lump forms in my throat. "Why? What's going on?"

He approaches me, dark circles under his eyes, salt-and-pepper hair standing on end. He pulls me into a hug. "Your mom was stabbed last night. She's been in surgery for hours." He takes a deep breath, and I still myself for the worst. "But she's going to be okay."

Relief slams into me. I grab on to my dad, and I hold him tighter than I've ever held anybody. Tears press my eyes.

"It's okay," he whispers.

I nod and, for the first time in my life, let tears fall.

He doesn't know what to do. He's never seen me cry. "It's okay," he murmurs. "You go ahead and give in."

I do. Letting tears fall freely. Giving in to the emotion I've never experienced before. He holds me tight, slightly rocking me, and I press my face into his chest.

Sometime later I blink and sniff, but he doesn't lessen his hold, and I realize he's crying too.

"What's going on?" Justin's voice interrupts us.

Slowly we pull apart and look down into his worried little-boy face.

Daisy comes down the stairs. "Who died?" she stupidly jokes.

I push past her and head up to my room. I'm *so* not in the mood for her right now.

In the background I hear Victor telling my brother and sister what he told me. They start crying, and I'm more than pleased that Daisy now knows what an idiot she is.

Later that morning our whole family sits around Mom's hospital bed. She's awake, but groggy.

Beside me, Justin hasn't stopped crying. This is the first time he's ever seen Mom like this, hooked to beeping equipment, IVs, tubes—defenseless.

It's the first time any of us have ever seen her less than strong, less than perfect.

Daisy sits across from us, clutching Mom's hand. It's the most affection I've seen her show Mom in a very long time.

A television hung on the wall is already reporting James Donner is a fraud and the Decapitator is still at large. There's footage of 4 Buchold Place, roped off now with police tape.

There's no mention of the Masked Savior. Maybe Mom hasn't gotten around to telling anybody yet. Or maybe she somehow figured out it's me. . . .

"Let me talk to Lane," Mom croaks. "Alone."

I give Justin a reassuring squeeze.

"Let's try to eat a little something," Victor says, and ushers my brother and sister out.

As the door closes, I scoot up beside Mom. "Are you in a lot of pain?"

She shakes her head, but I know she's lying. She licks her

dry lips, and I give her a couple of ice chips to suck on.

Mom closes her eyes and takes a few seconds like she's gathering her thoughts.

"Lane," she finally rasps. "You know this happened at Four Buchold Place, right?"

I nod. She must not have recognized me after all.

"Internally, the FBI is focusing on your uncle as the Decapitator."

Actually hearing the words in an official capacity renders me mute for a second. "What . . . what do you mean, internally?"

"Sometimes when an official announcement is made, it hinders the manhunt more than helps it. You need to be very careful. I have reason to believe the Decapitator, your uncle, is following me and probably you."

I have reason to believe it too. "What evidence is pointing in his direction?"

"I can't say. I'm sorry."

I try not to get frustrated. "Does the FBI know I own that house?"

"Of course they do. But they also know you have nothing to do with this."

If only that were true. "Where was your backup?"

She shakes her head. "He wanted me to come alone."

"Mom, that's stupid." Her machine beeps and I ignore it, watching her lick her dry lips again.

I give her more ice chips.

She sucks. "I've done it before, against FBI protocol, and gotten in trouble because of it."

This is news to me. And . . . doesn't sound like her at all. "Are you in trouble now?"

"I suspect so. My boss is coming to see me later."

"Was your team at least somewhere nearby?" *Did they see me?*

"You know I can't divulge details. And you must know your silence is imperative regarding your uncle. We can't afford to have any leaks."

I nod, trying to be the patient person I've always been but totally consumed by frustration.

With a soft groan she squints against the pain.

I touch her arm. "Can I get you anything?"

"I need to rest."

"Okay." I turn to leave.

"Lane?"

I turn back.

"I've put a guard on you. On the whole family. For a couple of weeks. I'm not taking any chances."

"What?" I can't have a guard. How in the hell am I supposed to operate with a guard on my ass?

Chapter Thirty

THE NEXT COUPLE OF DAYS GO BY AS expected—school and visiting Mom in the hospital.

Our FBI bodyguard is good at his job. I barely know he's there.

On Wednesday I get a text from a number I don't recognize.

HOW'D U LIKE ALMOST GETTING CAUGHT?

U SONOFABITCH, I bang back. U STABBED MY MOTHER!

AH, AND NOW WE KNOW WHAT FINALLY PENETRATES SLIM'S BARRIER.

I toss my phone on the bed and walk away from it. He knows he's gotten to me, and I despise that. All these years of thinking I had no family on my real dad's side, and the one I end up getting turns out to be a serial killer. And to think I'd been at first fascinated with him. . . . He stabbed my mother. I hate my uncle.

I snatch the phone back up and hit call. It rings once and I get the same "cannot be completed as dialed" message that I got before. I don't know why I bothered calling him back. I knew that would probably happen again.

The next afternoon I get home from the hospital and check the mail. Another small white envelope has been delivered with no return address.

My heart skips as I open up the envelope, already suspecting what I'll find. I pull out a pieced-together picture, similar to the other he sent, but now with a head, two arms, and a leg. The type below it reads:

ONE LEG TO GO.
I KNOW WHO THE FBI THINKS I AM.
AND THEY'RE WRONG.
MAYBE I'LL TELL YOU WHO I AM. *MAYBE*.
GOOD GIRL, KEEPING THIS TO YOURSELF.

I flip the card over, and there's a picture of my mom sitting in her car talking on her phone. Below the picture is:

LET'S HOPE I DON'T HAVE TO TEACH
ANYONE ELSE IN YOUR FAMILY A LESSON.

My jaw clenches as I flip the card back over and scan the lines again. *I know who the FBI thinks I am.* How does my uncle know that? Or maybe he doesn't and he's just playing with me. Either way we'll see how much of a *good girl* he thinks I am when I bust his ass.

I use the next couple of days to chart out his fourteen-year killing spree, starting with the woman I watched get stabbed to death.

I pick up the phone and call Reggie. "I know I said I didn't want you doing anything else with the Decapitator, but that bastard stabbed my mom."

"Oh, I've already been digging." Reggie really is a good and loyal friend.

"Okay. Couple of questions: Can you tell me where my real father has been over the past fourteen years in the month of September? Can you tell me where his brother, my uncle, has been? Can you tell me if either one of them was connected in any way to the women who have died, including that initial murder I witnessed? Finally, can you tell me who's been on and off the FBI task force over the past fourteen years? Specifically, Victor. I know he's traveled to many of the states where the killings occurred."

"Your stepdad. You don't think—"

"I'm not discounting anything. I'm on a warpath, and everyone connected to this in any way is game. I've lost all trust."

Through the phone I hear Reggie typing. "It's going to take me some time to put all this together."

"I know. And . . . I'd also like to know if I personally am connected to any of the fourteen women."

"What do you mean? Like, related?"

"Yeah, or anything else."

"Okay, I'll send things as I find them." With that, Reggie clicks off.

I pace my room, thinking through everything. Why would the Decapitator be contacting me personally if I don't have some sort of stake in all this?

Unless he thinks I saw him all those years ago, and he has to get rid of me as I'm the only eyewitness. So why lure me back to 4 Buchold? Is it his sick attempt at completing the killing cycle?

Or maybe he's after the whole family because my parents are on the investigative team.

Perhaps—and this is way out there—he fully intended to have me watch him all those years ago in order to make me into his successor.

Why, though, would he want a successor?

Reggie calls back. "There's no proof your father took you all those years ago. Everyone naturally assumed it since you were found at Four Buchold Place. He kidnaps you, you're found covered in blood, and no one thinks he committed that murder. It doesn't make sense. Something's off."

Something's *way* off. "I thought you said the reports noted he was questioned."

"They did. It's almost like the reports have been doctored or mistyped, or someone filed one and then someone else filed another. It's like there's—"

"Someone working on the inside." Like Victor.

"Exactly."

"So it could've been anyone who took me. Mom told me Seth and his brother both lived there."

"You're thinking your uncle might have kidnapped you?"

"It's possible." I pace across my bedroom. "Reggie, I honestly don't know. Just when I think I might have it figured out, I get confused again."

"Something else you should know. Your mom said your real father signed over rights to you, right?"

I stop pacing. "Let me guess. That's a lie."

Reggie sighs. "Sorry, Lane."

I promise you that's the last bit of information I kept from you. I promise. Mom's words come back to me, and I shake my head. Unbelievable.

I click off with Reggie and go straight downstairs to Mom's office. Victor's sitting at her desk. I don't even bother saying hi. "When did you adopt me?"

He looks up from the computer. "When you were three. Why?"

"Can I see the paperwork?"

"What's this all about?"

"I was looking through the paperwork that came from the

law firm," I lie. "My real father never signed over rights to me. Mom said he did."

He takes off his reading glasses. "Your Mom and I—"

"Just tell me the truth," I demand.

"Lane . . ."

I've never lost my temper with him. I've never taken that tone. It surprises me, too.

"I understand you're upset," he calmly responds. "Please know every decision we've made has been in your best interest."

I'm so sick of hearing that. "How is it in my best interest to continually lie to me?"

Victor pauses and I can see it all over his face. Guilt. Love. Exhaustion. Confusion. I want to understand, really I do, but I need honesty. Now.

"You're correct. Your real father never signed away rights to you. But that doesn't make you any less my daughter." He reaches for me. "I raised you. You *are* my own."

I ignore the tenderness that sparks inside me. "Why didn't he sign away rights to me?"

Victor takes my hand. "He said he wanted to. We spent years sending him paperwork only to have it returned undeliverable. Eventually we lost track of him altogether." He squeezes my fingers. "We can talk to Mom more about this when she gets out of the hospital if you want."

"I don't want to talk to Mom."

"Lane," he softly reprimands me. "Don't say that."

I don't respond as I stand in front him, no deflation at all in my frustration.

He lets go of my hand. "You have any more questions, you come to me. I'll be straight up with you."

I nod, even though deep down I know there's more. But, and I never thought I'd think this, in this moment I trust Victor more than my mom.

My past has scarred me for the future, and I have to be able to trust someone with that. The truth of the matter is, both my parents are trained liars. I can't trust either one.

"The woman you saw get stabbed to death was your preschool teacher," Reggie tells me.

I pull into Patch and Paw for my Saturday shift. No wonder I'd been clinging to her hand in the picture. "And the FBI hasn't worked this out?"

"I'm sure they have. But why would they tell you? Lane, your mom still doesn't know that you know about the murder you witnessed in that room. She saw you freak when you two visited Four Buchold. I'm sure if she knew I sent you that picture, she would've told you more details."

I doubt that. "Of course the woman I saw get killed was a preschool teacher. I can't believe I didn't think of that. That is the Decapitator's modus operandi."

"You can't think of everything."

"And the other women throughout the years? Am I con-nected to them in any way?"

"Not that I can see," Reggie answers. "As far as Seth and your uncle, it's hit or miss. The two of them are like ghosts. They're hard to track. They move around, sometimes together, sometimes separate. They seem to operate on cash only."

I turn my Jeep off. "Any connection to the women?"

"Just the first one being your teacher. None of the others, though. You're right about your stepdad. He's been on the investi-gative team for years."

"Longer than my mom?"

"Yes."

"How did I not know this? I feel like we've gotten nowhere."

"You don't think your stepdad is involved in some capacity other than investigative, do you?"

I sigh. "I don't know what to think. I'm frustrated. I'm con-fused. And I'm irritated as all hell. At this point I just want the Decapitator to come up and introduce himself to me."

"Lane, don't say that. A serial killer introducing himself? Please don't say that. I'm worried enough about you and your family as it is."

"You know I'm not being serious," I say to soothe her, even though I am.

Neither one of us says anything for a couple of seconds.

"Lane, promise me you'll be careful."

"I promise." And I will be careful, in my own distinctive way. We click off and I head inside.

"How's your mom?" Dr. Issa asks before I even set my stuff down.

"Fine. She comes home today." Everyone knows Mom's the lead investigator on the case. She's on the news frequently.

And everyone knows if she doesn't solve it soon, it'll be another year before the Decapitator strikes again and gives everyone another chance to catch him.

I pick up the work list, fully aware Dr. Issa is still standing, looking at me.

I turn. "Did you need something else?"

"Just . . . just wondering if you've talked to Zach."

"I'm not your brother's keeper," I snap.

Dr. Issa blinks in surprise.

I'm surprised too. I've lost my control more in the last few days than I have in my whole life.

"I know you're not my brother's keeper," he quietly responds. "I won't bring it up again."

With that, he's gone. I don't normally experience guilt about anything, but I do right now. Dr. Issa doesn't deserve my ire.

One thing is for sure. I've got to get back in control. It's the only way I know how to effectively function.

. . .

On my way home I swing by Giant to get a box of tampons, and see Zach standing in front of an ABC liquor store.

What the hell?

I don't get out of my Jeep and instead park and watch. He stands there for several good solid minutes and then opens the door and walks right inside.

What is he doing? There's no way they'll sell him liquor.

Time ticks by, and I continue watching the door, waiting, waiting . . . Several people come and go and still no Zach.

I open my Jeep and jump out. I'm going in after him. He's making a huge mistake. I don't know what's driven him in there, but he's going to regret it, big time.

The door opens and he strolls right out, no bags in hand. He catches sight of me standing in the middle of the parking lot, staring back at him. I do the only thing I can do. I lift my hand and wave.

He walks right toward me, and as I watch him approach, I make my mind up not to say a word. He knows I saw him. He should be the one to speak. Or not. It's not like he owes me an explanation.

"Busted." He laughs a little.

"What were you doing in there?" So much for me not saying anything.

"I do that sometimes. Go inside. Walk the aisles. It's reinforc-ing. It's challenging. My counselor at rehab suggested that, actu-ally."

"Oh. Well . . ."

"Were you worried?"

I think about that but don't immediately answer. And I don't bother reminding him he said he doesn't want to be friends.

He smiles—"Thanks"—and reaches out, surprising us both, and clasps my hand. The contact only lasts for a quick squeeze, and then he releases it. "See you at school." And with that, he turns and walks away.

I stand for a second watching his back. I like Zach. Seeing him nearly throw everything away makes me realize I like him more than I thought. Now what am I going to do about that?

Chapter Thirty-One

MOM COMES HOME ON SATURDAY AND
basically goes right to bed. Sunday we have a family day at our
house with movies, grilled burgers, and cards. Neither Victor
nor I mention our conversation to Mom. At this point I don't
want to bring anything else up. It will all be smothered in half
truths anyway.

By Monday Victor is back at work, Mom's still recuperating
at home, and I'm at school.

Zach comes up to me after the last period. "Hey, you."

My insides flutter a little at his unexpected appearance. My
reaction surprises me.

"Heard your mom came home."

"Yes."

"I'm happy."

"Thanks."

We both stand there for a second just looking at each other. I'm not really sure if he's waiting for me to say something else or not.

"Belinda's in rehab." He breaks the silence.

It takes me a second to digest the switch of topic. "Okay."

"I've been visiting her."

Of course he has. It's exactly what she wants. It's exactly the type of person he is. And one of the reasons why I like him.

"Anyway"—he glances around the hall—"that's all, I guess."

I close my locker and spin the dial. "Later, then."

I walk off, and even though I don't look back, I have the distinct sensation he's watching me. Just the thought of it makes my insides flutter again.

Our FBI watchdog follows us home. Daisy jumps on Facebook, Justin starts his homework, and, while I make a snack, I flip on the news.

"He's bold. I'll give him that much," one reporter comments. "Leaving the leg right in front of the FBI headquarters."

I freeze in my snack-making and stare at the television. They flash pictures of FBI headquarters and investigators milling about, and from far away some news crew has managed to snap a few photos of the shrink-wrapped leg.

"What happens if they don't catch that bad man?" Justin asks.

I grab the remote and flip the channel. I don't want Justin seeing this.

"What will happen?" Justin repeats.

He'll kill again. Next September. God knows where. "The FBI's going to catch him," I assure my brother, even though I highly doubt it.

The Decapitator will be delivering the hands and feet in a cooler soon, and that'll be the end of it.

Maybe he'll contact me next year when he starts up again. Or maybe he won't. Maybe this is my one and only chance to figure this puzzle out.

The office door opens and Mom storms out.

"I thought you were up in bed," I say. "I was just about to bring you a snack."

She slowly heads straight up the stairs. "Your dad's in charge of the case now."

Justin shoots me a look like he, too, has picked up on Mom's mood. I shake my head at him, and he nods his silent understanding.

This is the great thing about my brother. He's one of those go-with-the-flow kids. Now, if I had done that to Daisy, she would've flipped me off or given me choice words or any other million infuriating things.

I go find Mom. She's sitting in their window seat, staring out at the yard.

Quietly I take a seat beside her. "Are you saying you're not the director anymore?"

"No, I'm still the department's director. I still have other work, but I'm just not the lead on the Decapitator case."

"Does this have to do with the leg?"

She turns away from the window. "This has everything to do with the leg. And the fact I went to Four Buchold Place alone. And the fact your uncle is now the prime suspect."

The Decapitator basically flaunted his freedom right at FBI headquarters. I get it. "He's made your whole team look inadequate."

"Fresh eyes, fresh leadership is good," she diplomatically points out.

"Actually, I never knew you and Victor were working the same case."

"We weren't. But he's got a history with it, so he was a natural pick to step in."

"Is this going to cause problems between you two?"

"Of course not." Mom nods to her door. "Give me some time, please."

"Sure." As I leave, I hear her throw something across the bedroom. She's definitely pissed.

That night Victor's not even at dinner, and Mom barely speaks.

As I'm looking through my homework, I get a text from a

number I don't recognize. MAYBE YOUR STEPDAD WILL HAVE BETTER LUCK.

I don't bother responding and instead work on my assignment.

About thirty minutes later, he's texting me again. I GET IT. I'M ANNOYING U. GOOD.

I turn my phone off. He's right. He's annoying me.

I go to bed early, and as I'm drifting off to sleep, I register Victor coming in and giving me a kiss good night. He smells like alcohol, and in that sleep/dream haze I mumble, "Sure you should be drinking?"

"Just a glass of wine," he whispers and touches the tip of my nose with his index finger. It's been so long since he's done that. Like years, I think.

I wonder if he *will* have better luck than my mom.

The next morning in first period Reggie texts me. YOUR OLD PRESCHOOL TEACHER & SETH WERE DATING.

And the FBI didn't know this? Surely they knew something that huge.

But . . . that explains why she was at 4 Buchold Place. It doesn't explain how she became the first victim.

At lunch the assistant principal finds me in the cafeteria. "Lane, your mom called. She wants you to come home right now."

I stand up. "What about Daisy?"

"She said just you."

I throw my half-eaten burrito away, get my stuff from my locker, and, as I drive home, try to call Mom. She doesn't pick up. Panic has me immediately dialing back. It goes straight to voice mail, and I gun my engine. My brain's going about a million worried miles an hour when I race into our house. "Mom?"

I go to the office first, find it empty, and head straight upstairs.

She's sitting at my desk, my laptop on, my room turned upside down around her.

"Sit down," she orders, not even glancing up.

She pulls up the password-protected nanny-cam footage first. Then all the password-protected files and the text message log. Beside my laptop sit the small white no-return-address envelopes I've hidden under my mattress.

Mom finally looks at me. "I knew you were hiding something from me."

She's one to talk.

"How'd you figure out my passwords?"

She shoots me a glance like that's the most ridiculous question I could've asked. There's something to be said for having FBI parents. Pretty much nothing can be kept a secret.

She motions to the laptop, to the envelopes. "He's been contacting you?"

"Obviously."

She narrows her eyes in warning. "Explain yourself, young lady."

"I don't know why he's been contacting me, but I've been playing things out."

"*Playing things out?* This isn't a game."

"I know that."

"You nanny-cammed my office?"

"I was desperate. Reggie wasn't willing to hack your computer."

Mom just looks at me. "I don't know who you are, but I can't trust you."

I pull up the picture of me at three years old holding my teacher's bloody hand. "And I can't trust you. What else are you keeping from me?"

Mom shakes her head. "I can't believe it's turned into this between you and me."

I'm not sorry. She's just as guilty as I am. I point to the picture. "You knew what happened to me at Four Buchold and you didn't tell me. You watched me have that horrible flashback and acted all innocent like you had no clue. *I* don't know who *you* are." I'm glad to throw that back in her face.

"You were there the night I got stabbed," she accuses me. "That was you, wasn't it?"

"Yes."

"And you left me there."

It wasn't like that.

She huffs. "What, were you afraid the *Masked Savior* was going to get busted?"

I don't bother denying my other identity.

"Do you have any idea how *dangerous* this secret life of yours is?"

"I'm careful."

"You're just a teenage girl!"

"What? Are you saying you're worried for me?"

"Of course I'm worried!"

Yeah, but she didn't actually say it until I prompted her. "You seem more angry."

"Yes, angry!" She holds up a flash drive. "I'll be turning these files, the text communication, and the envelopes over to the FBI. I will not be giving them the nanny-cam footage or the fact that you wear a ski mask and fight crime." She stands up. "You and I will deal with that later when I've calmed down."

"Well, I'm angry too!" I fire back.

At my doorway she turns and glares at me. "I want you to think about this. If you had handed this information over as you got it, we would've caught this horrible killer by now. Do you realize how many hours have gone into looking for your uncle?" She holds up the last communication I got from him and reads, "'I know who the FBI thinks I am and they're wrong.' According to that statement it may not even be him.

But because of you and your sick curiosity, another person is probably going to die."

Her words send prickly chills racing across my neck.

"*And* I am making an appointment for you with a psychiatrist. There is something not right with you and, frankly, it scares me."

Chapter Thirty-Two

OVER THE NEXT FEW DAYS I BARELY SEE Victor, and my mom only speaks to me when absolutely necessary.

Her underlying hostility and extreme disappointment unnerve me.

Because of you and your sick curiosity, another person is probably going to die.

Is that what I have—sick curiosity? It doesn't seem sick and unnatural. It's such a part of me I can't imagine it not being there. Between my abusive grandfather, my real father who killed him, and my uncle the possible Decapitator, darkness *is* my heritage. If I had expected to receive understanding from anybody, it would have been my mother.

Now I know that's not the case. She thinks I'm unbalanced right along with everyone else, if they knew my innermost thoughts.

Aside from all that, I craved to get out, to hunt somebody. I itched for it. I longed for it. I wanted, no *needed*, to bring someone down and have adrenaline swelling my veins again.

On Thursday night I purposefully stay up until Victor comes home. He's yet to say a word to me since Mom ransacked my bedroom.

Having one parent pissed at me is one thing, but two? Too much. I formed a life around not caring what others think. The truth is, my parents' opinions of me matter, even if they both agree I'm sick.

Victor tosses his keys onto the hallway table and raises his red, tired eyes to mine. "Hey, what are you still doing up?"

"Waiting on you."

"Oh?"

"Are we . . . Are we okay?"

He scrunches his brows. "What are you talking about?"

I let a significant amount of time pass as I wait for him to realize what I'm referring to.

Finally he shakes his head. "Lane, baby, I'm so tired. Can we do this in the morning?"

"Sure."

With a nod and a stifled yawn, he shuffles upstairs. I watch him go, completely puzzled. For all intents and purposes, he seems as if he doesn't even know what Mom found in my room. She said she would be handing everything over to the FBI. Maybe she changed her mind. Or perhaps she did hand everything over, and Victor just isn't ready to deal with me personally on the issue. And if she did hand everything over, surely someone official will be questioning me. Unless the FBI is leaving that up to my Mom and stepdad to handle.

The next morning in first-period library I pull up my e-mail. In my inbox are several from Belinda. I consider deleting them unopened, then notice they have pictures attached.

Curiosity wins out and I click on the first one. It's a picture of her and Zach, grinning with their cheeks smooshed together.

The second one shows them kissing, tongues and all.

The third one shows them having sex, her on top.

The fourth one shows her giving him a hand job.

I don't bother opening the others. I can only imagine.

The last e-mail has no attachment and so I bring it up. It says simply: *Glad to have him back and* inside *me.*

What a disgusting girl.

I do something out of character and forward them all to Zach with my message: *Thought you'd like to see what your* ex *is passing along.*

As I mentioned before, I don't do drama. It's not my thing.

But I like Zach and, bottom line, Belinda's not treating him right.

After school it doesn't surprise me when he finds me in the parking lot. "Can we talk?"

I toss Daisy my keys, and she rolls her eyes.

"Hurry, would you?" she whines.

I turn to Zach, ignoring my idiotic sister. "What's up?" I know what's up, of course.

He leads me a few steps away and keeps his voice low. "Those pictures were taken over a year ago. I had no clue she had a camera set up in her room. We were both drunk, as I've mentioned we always were."

I nod. "Okay."

"Okay?"

"You don't have to explain." Really, what does he want me to say?

He shakes his head. "I'm totally embarrassed that you saw those. I'm mortified. It's just like her to do that too. I hope you know I didn't have any cameras when we . . . ya know."

"Had sex?" Why do people find that act a challenge to admit or say in everyday conversation? Especially between two people who have participated in said act.

"God, Lane, yeah, had sex." Zach looks around.

"And yet you're visiting her in rehab," I point out.

"She's not in rehab anymore. She gave up."

Figures.

"Despite what you think—"

"I don't think anything," I interrupt.

"Despite what you think, I didn't get back together with her. I was just trying to be a good friend. You have no idea how hard it is to go through rehab."

"You're right, I don't." I glance back at the Jeep to see Daisy impatiently waving me on.

"I'm sorry you got hurt in all this," he quietly says.

"I didn't get hurt."

"Yes," he knowingly acknowledges, "you did."

No, I didn't.

He rakes his fingers through his dark hair, which, I notice, is starting to curl a bit. "See ya around, Lane." With that he turns and heads off across student parking.

I watch him go. Okay, he's right. I did get hurt—a little. I lost a friend I'd barely gotten to know. I lost a guy I realized I was starting to genuinely like.

Daisy honks the horn, and I resist the urge to flip her off. I climb in and drive off, glad she's got the music cranked. I don't feel like listening to her bullshit.

That night after dinner I get an encrypted e-mail from an unknown sender. I click around, try to figure out how to open it, and come up with nothing. About thirty minutes later my cell buzzes from a number I don't recognize. pw: jg41ost. I go back to the encrypted message, type in the password, and up pops a video.

It's dark and I lean in to make it out. A light flicks on and I see a blond woman, gagged, naked, and strapped to a table. There is no sound, and I watch as she stares off to the right, shaking, yanking against her holds.

A person steps into view, but his image has been doctored and is blurred. He pulls out a long knife, more like a sword, and its edge glints in the light.

I ignore him for a second and zero in on the woman's face. She's the latest Decapitator's victim. This is an old video. He's sent me the kill room.

With the graininess of the film, I can't place the room, but I'm sure it's not 4 Buchold Place. However, something about it *does* seem familiar. . . .

I turn my attention back to him. He circles the table to the top and braces his hand on her forehead. While she violently thrashes, he puts the knife to her neck and with long—slow—thorough—slices—takes her head right off.

It plunks to the floor, and I inhale sharply.

He moves to her hands next, taking them both off with a single chop, and then does the same to her feet.

He lays the knife on her torso and disappears from view. While he's out of view, I study the blood pumping from her body. There's so much. And it's creating a pool beneath the table.

Seconds later he comes back with a small white cooler and packs her hands and feet on ice. This is the same cooler he'll be sending to the police, I'm sure. I watch his every movement. Something seems different about him. He seems heavier than before and a bit taller. I try to back the video up, but it won't allow me to. Perhaps the camera has moved a bit and distorted his image even more. Perhaps *he's* distorted his image even more in an attempt to throw me further off.

I put that thought aside and watch as he slices her right arm off, then her left, but both arms stay strapped to the table.

He takes her legs off at the hip with the same slow, thorough slices he used on her head. Like the arms, the legs stay strapped to the table.

While he methodically cleans and resharpens the knife, I focus on the cut lines and the blood continuing to drain from the woman's body.

It's all very organized and methodical. And despite the amount of blood, it comes across as clean.

He pulls out a hose and begins washing everything down. Where is it going—a drain of some sort? It has to be, because the previously pooled blood and accumulating water disappear as he rinses.

Eventually he'll wrap the pieces in airtight plastic for preservation. I stare at the screen, waiting to see how he goes about this.

Then suddenly everything goes black. I lean in.

Yellow type appears on the screen:

IF YOU WATCHED THIS
AND FELT ONLY FASCINATION . . .
IF YOU WANTED MORE . . .
THEN YOU'RE READY.
P.S. I HAVE A PRESENT FOR YOU.

The video goes away and I feverishly click, trying to bring it back up, but it won't relaunch.

The video is all I can think about the rest of the weekend. I *had* watched it with complete fascination, emotionally detached, almost from an impartial medical viewpoint.

I did experience distress for the woman—a person who has been dead now several weeks. Perhaps if I'd known the individual on that table I would've felt different.

Then you're ready, the yellow type had said. Ready for what—to be a killer?

P.S. I have a present for you. Another video, pictures, more mail? And when will this present come—today, tomorrow, a week from now?

Because of you and your sick curiosity, another person is probably going to die.

My mom's words echo through my brain. She's right. I am sick.

Because I *am* interested to see what my present is. Only a sick person would be interested in a present from a serial killer. I realize that. But I *am* full of nothing but disdain for this man, present or not. He's twisted and malicious and deserves nothing less than death.

I'll give Mom the video link tonight, even though it probably won't launch again, and let her pass it along to the FBI team.

"What's wrong with you?" Daisy scowls from the passenger side of my Jeep. "You're even more quiet than usual."

I shake my head—"Just thinking"—and round the corner onto our campus.

Police cars have swarmed the place, and we're being directed to continue on.

Daisy sits forward. "What the—?"

Several blocks down we see students' cars parked alongside the road, and we pull over.

Daisy jumps out. "Gunman? Bomb? What is it?"

Crying, one of her cheerleading friends hugs her. "There was a cooler with hands and feet in it."

So the Decapitator decided to deliver the hands and feet to my school. Some present.

Daisy starts crying too.

My cell buzzes. There's a picture attached, and I pull it up to see the cooler propped open, with a pair of hands on display and red-painted toenails on both feet.

LIKE YOUR PRESENT?

Chapter Thirty-Three

HUMAN NATURE HAS ALWAYS PERPLEXED me. People cry even when they don't know the person they're crying for.

This is what goes through my mind as I stand amid all the students at school the next day, sad, hugging, and visiting grief counselors over the hands and feet of a woman they didn't even know.

The Decapitator has broken routine by delivering the cooler to a school. In all the reports I read, he delivers it to a police station. This was a present for me, although no one knows this information but myself. And so I decide to tell my mom. I would tell Victor, but he's barely around the house anymore.

"A present for you," my mom states.

S. E. GREEN

"Yes."

"Why would the Decapitator think that cooler is a present for you?"

"Why would the Decapitator do anything he's doing? The FBI knows I own Four Buchold. That I witnessed a murder there. And the Decapitator is somehow connected to me. What is the problem with finding him? I'm assuming you all still think it's my uncle?" Even I can hear the agitation in my tone.

My mom sighs. "It's not that easy."

"He'll be moving on soon. It'll be next September before he kills again."

"We know that, Lane. Don't you think we know that? And I want you to know that Seth and your uncle were in every state when the decapitations occurred."

This I already know because of Reggie's information. "So, what, are you saying they were working together?" I immediately recall the video. Maybe it *had* been two people and not just a different camera angle.

"I can't say anything else."

I growl. "Then why say anything at all? What about the video? Were you able to open that?"

"I *won't* say anything else."

I continue grilling her, even though she's closed down on me. "Why would they let you investigate all this with my real father and uncle being so closely tied?"

230

"I was already working the case before we realized all the connections. It doesn't matter; a true FBI professional can compartmentalize and focus."

"Is that why you went off half-cocked and got pulled from the case?"

"That's enough," she snaps at me. "I am still your mother, and you will speak to me with respect." With that she disappears into her office and slams the door.

I stand for several solid seconds, fuming at that closed door. I would love to go in there and fire back at her.

A movement in my peripheral vision has me whipping around.

Daisy holds her hands up. "Easy."

I get right in her face instead. "I swear to God, if you mess with me, I will—"

Her eyes widen. "I won't mess with you. I promise."

I take a step back and turn away. As much as I can't stand my sister, I don't have the right to take this out on her. This is my shit. Not hers.

"I . . . I was hungry and thought I'd make spaghetti for everyone. That's all."

I nod but don't look at her, and after several minutes of hearing her move around in the kitchen, I go to help.

I can't remember the last time Daisy and I made dinner together. What kind of sisters are we? Basically, we're strangers living in the same house. When all this is over, I should make more of an effort with her. Try to find some common ground. I mean, does she think I like not liking her?

"I wish this whole thing would go away," she grumbles later into her spaghetti.

"Cramping your style?"

She looks up at me and laughs. "Something like that."

I smile back. It's been so long since she and I have been friends.

"I know we don't know that lady, that teacher who died, but . . . will you go to the memorial service with me tomorrow?"

I hadn't planned on it, but the fact Daisy just asked me has me answering, "Sure."

"Do you think he'll deliver something to my school?" Justin whispers.

Daisy and I shoot each other a glance, and in that second it strikes me how much my depravity has affected my younger brother. I don't know why the Decapitator has chosen me. If he *is* my uncle, being his niece can't be the sole reason. I would think there's got to be something else.

What I do know is that if I had given everything over to the FBI from the start, he would be caught by now.

And my younger brother, who I love more than anybody, wouldn't be sitting here sad, worried about horrible things like body parts.

Daisy reaches over and tenderly strokes his cheek. "Of course not. It's all over now."

It's not, though.

That night Justin's nightmare wakes the whole house. I lie in bed, listening to him scream, listening to my parents run into his room, listening to him cry.

He sleeps with them, as does Daisy, and I stay right in my bed, laden with guilt.

The next day at school goes the same way with grief counselors and all, and after dinner Daisy and I leave for the memorial service.

"I've never been to a funeral," she whispers as we park outside the church.

I give her a bolstering look that I myself don't even feel.

"I heard they waited for all her body parts to have the memorial service. Isn't that sad?"

Yes, it's very sad.

We enter the packed place, and I have to admit there are more people here than I expected.

As I take a seat next to Daisy and look around, it occurs to me how many people come to these things to support the family.

Sure the congregation is full of kids from our school, here, I'm sure, like Daisy. Not because they knew the preschool teacher, but because the tragedy brought them in, and because this happened to someone in our community. And then there are those here, I'm sure, out of some weird fascination.

But the majority is adults—friends of the family, people they probably work with, extended relatives.

Up front sits a large portrait of a smiling woman. Staring at the picture, I can see how the Decapitator had been drawn to her pretty sweetness. It's curious how portraits come across so innocent.

On a wall in our house our parents have school pictures of each of us kids. They update them every year. Justin's always grinning, Daisy's got a pretty smile, and my expression remains blank. I wonder what people think of those when they see them. They probably think I'm the "difficult" child.

The service progresses, people speak, someone sings. When the whole thing is over, we head outside to see news crews camped out.

Of course I didn't know this woman, but I experience a flash of aggravation at their presence.

"What was it like to finally have her hands and feet delivered?" An obnoxious reporter gets right in the victim's family's face.

A woman around my mom's age crumbles, and a man angrily shoves the camera. "Have some respect."

As Daisy and I climb into my keyed Wrangler, I look up and see Dr. Issa across the church parking lot. He's looking right at me.

I give him an acknowledging wave, and he returns that with a nod before climbing in his Juke and pulling away. I wonder if he knew the preschool teacher and that's why he's here.

Later that night I go into Daisy's room to see how she's doing—something I haven't done in a very long time—and she's not there.

I look around upstairs and then head down. "Justin, seen Daisy?"

He doesn't even bother glancing up from his coloring books. "Nope."

I try her phone next. Its musical ring echoes from upstairs. I head up and into her room just as it stops playing. I dial again and locate it under the dress she wore to the memorial service.

Daisy never goes anywhere without her cell.

A chilly breeze races across my skin, and I glance over to her open window. A tiny slit is the only sign it's been opened and not reclosed all the way.

I walk over, lift it up, and stick my head out. The rolled

fire escape ladder Victor makes us keep in our rooms dangles down the side of the house.

Unbelievable. This is not the time for her to take off with one of her many guys.

West was the last one's name, and so I find him in our student directory and dial his number. "This is Lane, Daisy's sister."

"Oh, hey, Slim."

I don't even know this guy. "Is she with you?"

"No, she's at that girl's funeral."

No, she's not. "You guys are still together, right?" I never know with her. "She wouldn't be with someone else?"

"She better *not* be with someone else," he fires back.

I take a patient breath. "Don't worry about it. I'm looking for her. That's all."

"Try her phone."

A real genius, this one. "Thanks, I'll do that. Tell her to call me if you two talk."

I click off and start going through the student directory, calling all her cheerleading friends.

An hour later I've gotten nowhere.

"Be back in a sec," I tell Justin as I head to the front door.

Across the street sits our FBI guy. He's staring right at me, like he thinks I'm going to run or something. He should've been staring this way at Daisy while she shimmied out the back.

I take a few steps toward him, and my phone vibrates. Sliding my hand across the screen, I unlock it and a video pops up.

Zach. Strapped to a table. Shaking. Naked. Gagged. Eyes wide with fear. The message below says:

TELL ANYONE AND HE DIES.

Chapter Thirty-Four

I HEAD BACK INSIDE THE HOUSE AND straight up to my room. I take a seat at my desk and pull up the fifteen-second video of Zach on my phone. Like the other one, there is no sound.

I stare at his shaking body and my muscles tense. Watching the other video had mesmerized me. Watching this one terrifies me. Zach means a lot to me. More than I ever realized.

Closing my eyes, I inhale one long, cleansing breath and let it out slow.

My eyes reopen and I focus on the room he is in. I'm absolutely sure it's not 4 Buchold Place.

On my laptop I try to bring up the other video, but the link is still expired. From my memory it is the identical room.

Wherever my uncle killed that woman, he is now holding Zach. And the fact he's allowing me to watch Zach's video more than once—it's like he's toying with me.

I dial Reggie. "Other than Four Buchold Place, did my real father or uncle own anything else?"

"Just a sec." I hear her clicking her keyboard. "Doesn't look like it."

"How about did they live anyplace else near here?"

"No, that's the only address that shows up for them in your area."

I sit back. Focus. Think. *In my area* . . . "How about outside the area? Like Maryland?"

She click, click, clicks. "Sorry, no."

"Okay."

A knock sounds on my door, and my mom sticks her head in. "Wanted you to know I'm home. But only for a minute."

"Hang on," I tell Reggie, and focus back on my mom.

"Dad's still at the office, and I'm heading back there, actually."

"I thought you got pulled off the case?"

"I did. But there are other investigations I'm manning."

"Were you all ever able to open that video?"

Her expression softens. "I'm so sorry you had to see that."

My pulse quickens. "You *were* able to pull it up?"

"Yes, and I'm so sorry you had to see it," she repeats.

I'm dying to ask her how they got the video to relaunch but of course can't. "Did it help?" I ask instead.

"It has. They've been able to figure out a lot of things we were unsure of."

Like what—where the kill room is? Where Zach is? "Mom—"

Tell anyone and he dies.

"Yes?"

I want to tell her about Zach. I want to get her help. But I know I can't. Zach will die if I don't do what the Decapitator wants. "Nothing," I mumble.

Some awkward seconds pass.

"Thank you"—she breaks the awkwardness—"for listening to me. For not keeping more information from me. I should've told you that earlier."

"Sure." At least I've earned back a teeny bit of her trust. Which will all be gone again as soon as she realizes I'm keeping Zach a secret.

"Okay, I have to go back. I only came home to grab some files." She nods to my phone. "And you have a conversation to finish." She gives me a slight wave and closes my door behind her.

I go back to Reggie. "Sorry about that. So what did you find?"

"Well, when you said Maryland, a bell dinged in my head. I remember your mom talking about Gaithersburg, Maryland, and how you all lived there before moving to McLean."

The memory hits me. "That's right. I'd forgotten all about that. I think I was in second grade when we moved."

"Anyway, your stepdad still owns the house."

"What? Why?"

"He rents it out."

"Who's in it right now?"

"No one. It's been empty for a few months."

I grab a pen and paper and notice my hands are shaking. I ignore them and focus. "Give me the address."

We hang up, and someone knocks on my door. "Lane?"

Daisy? I swing the door open and pull my sister into a hug. "Where the hell have you been?"

It takes her a second to realize we're hugging. "The tree house."

I pull back. "Do *not* leave this house. Got me?"

"Sorry," she mumbles, and it occurs to me that a week ago she would've cussed me out over that demand. "I'm going to be in my room," she says, and shuffles off.

I watch her for a second, completely elated and overcome by the fact she's fine. After she closes her bedroom door, I close my own, open my window, and go out the same way Daisy did—down the retractable ladder.

I sprint through our side yard to where my Jeep is parked along the curb and plug the Maryland address into my GPS. *Hang on, Zach. Hang on. . . .*

I jump on 495, and forty-five minutes later I arrive at my childhood house. I park several blocks down and sit for a second, surveying the area. Memories rush back and I reel at their onslaught. Pedaling my bike. Playing in the leaves. Making brownies for a block party.

It's a cute neighborhood—what my parents would call starter homes. A bike rests against a tree in one yard. A plastic toddler wagon sits upside down on a porch. Halloween lights and decorations blink through front windows.

Kid friendly. Safe. Great place to raise a family. Great place to hide Zach.

No one would guess the Decapitator has him just a few blocks down.

Quickly I slip my cargo pants on over my skinny jeans and pack the pockets with my supplies. I don't bother with my ski mask—the Decapitator knows what I look like.

The street is well lit, but it's getting late and no one's out. Still, there's no hiding in shadows as I race for my old house and Zach. If someone was to drive by, they'd assume I was out for a late run.

The small Cape Cod is dark, making it seem as if no one lives here. Laughter echoes through my memories, and I have a flash of Daisy racing across the yard, her blond braids flying, Mom chasing her.

This is the house I lived in when I was taken at three years old.

My thoughts trail off as my brain makes connections between Victor and this house—he's been in all the states where the decapitations occurred, he has the ability to cover up records. He could be in on this whole thing.

I stop for a second and glance around the small yard, tended bushes, tiny porch, rolled-up water hose, and decorative brick walkway. How did the Decapitator get Zach past all this and inside? Surely a neighbor would have seen someone carrying a body indoors. Then again, probably not. The Decapitator's good. He would know how to get a body inside without stirring suspicion.

I take in the stone birdbath to the left and suddenly, very distinctly, recall our neighbor building it.

Beyond the birdbath and around the corner of the house sits the kitchen door off the driveway. I automatically move toward it, instinct directing me, in the way a person does out of habit.

The front door always got jammed, I remember now, and so we would use the side kitchen door.

I reach for the knob and turn it, not surprised at all to find it unlocked. It swings open, and I stand staring into the dark kitchen.

He's here. I can *feel* him.

I step over the threshold, close the door behind me, and stand reorienting myself to the place.

A combination of moonlight and light from the streetlamps filters through the blinds and casts an intermittent glow here and there.

I experience a quick flash of Victor standing by the stove, flipping pancakes. This place seems full of nothing but good and happy memories. Now it'll be full of anything but.

Beyond the kitchen spans the living room and past that the master bedroom. Two smaller ones lie to the left, separated by a bathroom.

Daisy and I shared the farthest one away, and so I head straight there.

A light flickers from the crack beneath the door. The Decapitator's in there. Zach's in there, strapped to a table, scared, fighting for what seconds of life he has left.

Zach's presence, the Decapitator's presence, they both fill me, overwhelm me in an intense single-mindedness that I welcome. The Decapitator will die for this. I *will* kill him and end his life of terror.

I unbutton my cargo pockets, ready to grab whatever I need, and reach for the doorknob.

With a twist I give it a slight push, and it slowly swings inward.

Large sheets of black plastic cover every inch of the ceiling, walls, and floor. On an examining table in the center lies Zach, unconscious and strapped down.

No one else is in the room. A small lamp sitting on the floor provides the only light.

Crossing the plastic, I go to him and test the canvas straps. I'll have to cut them off. I take in his slack face, shallow breaths, and pale skin. What has he been drugged with? I glance around the table and underneath it, where the black plastic disappears through a cutout portion of the flooring. This must be the drain I saw on the video. I don't understand. Did the Decapitator burrow a hole right through the house's floor? And where does it go to—a drain line of some sort, the septic tank, dirt beneath the house?

In my peripheral vision I catch movement and automatically reach for my Taser. I yank it from my pocket, turn, and freeze.

The Decapitator nods. "Hello, Lane. Welcome."

Chapter Thirty-Five

"MOM?"

She comes toward me, takes the Taser from my hand, and backs away. "You're the daughter I was meant to have."

I glance quickly to Zach, then right back to my mom. "I don't . . . I don't understand."

She props her shoulder in the doorway and folds her arms across her chest. "What don't you understand, daughter?"

Is she for real? "How about *everything*?" I point to Zach. "Why haven't you helped him?"

Mom spares him a quick glance. "I was saving him for you. For us. I want to do him together."

Do him together?

"Oh, don't act like you didn't know."

I didn't!

"Do you realize how great we'll be together?" Mom keeps going as if we're having a normal conversation.

"Decapitating people?"

She smiles. "With my position in the FBI and your innate talents . . . We'll be great. We'll go down in history as the most infamous serial killers never caught. Besides, now that Seth is dead, I need another partner."

This takes a second to sink in. "I'm sorry, what?"

"Well, you didn't think I could pull all this off by myself. Honestly"—she chuckles—"I'm good, but I'm not that good."

My brain spirals with questions, with memories, with facts, but I don't have the time to give them space to unravel. I need to focus. "You two killed my preschool teacher?"

"She was fucking your dad. It pissed me off. I walked right in on them. *We* walked right in on them."

I've never heard my mom drop the f-bomb. It comes across so foreign . . . and ridiculous. "But you were already married. . . . And what do you mean, *we*?"

"Seth was and always will be my one true love."

I shake my head. She's making no sense. "Then why get married?"

"Because Seth can be a real asshole, and I had to teach him

a lesson. I like to hold my *happy* marriage over his head. But then I got pregnant with Daisy and my job at the FBI, and well, here I am, all these years later."

"What do you mean, *we*?" I repeat. "Who took me? Who kidnapped me when I was three?"

"Nobody. It's the story we made up. I took you to Four Buchold. Seth had no clue we were coming. We walked right in on him and that bitch. That's when it all went down. I grabbed a knife from the kitchen and stabbed her, then stabbed again, and then Seth joined in." She huffs an unamused laugh. "You watched the whole thing."

I get really still.

"You just stood there mesmerized by what we were doing."

My whole body chills. "I was not," I whisper.

She nods. "You were. You wouldn't look away."

Anger surges through my blood, turning my chilled body into a furnace. "I was in shock!"

"It was your idea that we cut off her head, arms, and legs."

Bile swells into my throat, and I swallow the overwhelming desire to heave. "That's a lie."

Mom shakes her head. "No, it's not."

Yes it is! It has to be a lie!

"That first kill was our crime of passion, and—it did something to us. When you stood there and watched, we knew you were feeling it too."

All the air in my lungs leaves me. "And all those other women?" I whisper.

Mom shrugs. "Yearly celebration of our first kill." Her face brightens. "You don't understand how thrilling it is for Seth and me. There's nothing like it."

I can't hear any more.

She shakes her head. "Do you know how many hours, days, weeks, months, *years* the FBI has put into this? Trying to figure the Decapitator—*us*—out?" She laughs. "Ridiculous."

I eye this woman, my mother, a person I don't even know. "How'd you pick your victims?"

"Preschool teachers, blondes . . ."

I trusted you. I admired you. I respected you. I wanted to be like you. All these things pop into my mind, but I say none of them. "What about your husband? What about Justin? And Daisy?"

"Don't you see? They'll have each other. You and I will have each other. We'll be the perfect family. Besides"—she nods to Zach—"now that Seth's gone we need something new. New victims, new techniques. We need to make this *us* now."

"He's my friend," I whisper.

"No. He's not. If he were your friend, he wouldn't have turned his back on you."

"He didn't."

"I have an itch that needs scratching, and he's going to do it."

I don't like that she's used "itch." That's my word.

"He's a present. For you."

Who is this woman who has terrorized others for fourteen years? I barely recognize her. It's like I'm meeting her for the first time tonight.

She moves finally, pushing away from the door, and my whole body tenses. "Be back in a sec," she tells me.

Mom disappears, and I quickly look around, my brain in overdrive. How am I going to get me and Zach out of here?

Wait. My tranquilizer gun!

Mom reappears in that exact second holding something behind her back.

I've never once felt the urge to retreat from anything or anybody, but the need to back up, even one step, overcomes me.

Zach mumbles and stirs.

Don't wake up, Zach. Don't wake up.

With a smile, Mom pulls a long knife from behind her back. I recognize it from the video.

The video . . .

She and Seth sliced that woman and packaged her parts, and I watched with fascination, with *sick curiosity*, just as Mom claimed.

Maybe she's right. Maybe this is my destiny. But . . . how can this be my destiny if they created it by allowing me to watch, by making me *participate* all those years ago?

They made me into this indescribable, abnormal, distorted person. If it weren't for their twisted delight, I'd be a normal seventeen-year-old girl. Happy. Functional. Emotional at times. Bright. Adjusted.

Mom moves close to Zach, trailing the sharpened blade along the table. "You should have seen us the first couple of times. A dull blade does not make for a very clean kill."

I hate her. I really hate her. "What about my uncle?"

She laughs. "You don't have an uncle. We made him up just in case the FBI ever got too close."

"But . . . you can't just make a person up."

"Lane, baby, do you realize who I am? Do you realize the resources I have access to? I've spent my adult life hunting people. I can certainly make one up. I know how to generate false paperwork and make it look perfect."

"But he stabbed you."

"I stabbed myself."

But I heard two people fighting . . . or did I? "Why would you stab yourself?"

She laughs. "It's all a game, Lane. I had to make it look like your uncle was there, not only for the FBI, but for you. Just like the different-colored hair—part of the game. Every other year we'd color the victim's hair to throw things off."

"What about all the information I gave you that you passed on to . . ." Suddenly realization dawns. She never passed any of the information on to the investigative team.

Mom chuckles at my realization. "See what I mean? I'm the perfect person to have on your side."

Numbly I stare at her, wishing she would've died by her own stab wound. "And all the text messages threatening me, threatening my—*our*—family?"

"Manipulation. Needed you to do what I wanted you to do."

"You leaked all that information to the press, didn't you?"

"Yes. All calculated for an end result."

"And James Donner?"

She shakes her head. "Stupid idiot. Wasn't expecting that one. But I like a good challenge. He livened things up. He'd done his research. He actually knew one of the victims. That's how he knew nail-polish color."

"Nail polish . . ." I don't understand.

"It's the one detail we leave out of reports. It's our way of double-checking copycats and verifying false leads." She rounds the table and glances up at me, tears suddenly in her eyes. "I miss Seth. Colon cancer ran in his family. You need to make sure you get checked in a few years. Okay, sweetheart?"

I stare at her.

"Okay?" she repeats.

"Okay," I robotically agree.

"I'm so glad he came back home to die. I'm so glad we got

one last kill." She slides the knife's tip along Zach's throat and draws a tiny sliver of blood.

"Mom."

She looks up.

I slip my hand into the pocket where the tranquilizer gun lies loaded and ready.

She glances down to my hand. "Yes?"

I reach out from my pocket empty-handed. "May I?"

She cocks her head. "Really?"

"Really."

"Okay." She lays the handle in my palm. "Okay."

I test the weight of it as the images of those fourteen women flash through my mind.

Trust. Mom has so easily given it to me by handing me the knife.

Trust. It's what Zach has that someone will rescue him.

Trust. The whole nation has it that the FBI will bring the Decapitator to justice.

Trust. I've always, naturally, given it to my mom.

"DO IT!" she screams.

Her cry ricochets across my nerve endings. I whip around and take her head off with one slice.

Her body falls limp to the floor, and I drop to my knees.

I am my mother's daughter.

I am a killer.

Epilogue

I HAVE NO CLUE HOW LONG I'VE BEEN KNEEL-
ing, but Zach's watch dings and I lift my head. I glance at my mom
first, at her headless body curled in her own pool of blood and at
her head that has rolled to the corner of the room. The eyes on that
head stare at the ceiling. I'm grateful they are not looking at me.

I notice her blood is creeping in my direction, and I get to
my feet. Zach stirs then and I straighten. *I can't let him see this.* I
glance around the room, looking for I'm not sure what, and my
gaze narrows in on the cloth shoved in Zach's mouth. I slip it
out and quickly tie it around his eyes.

He mumbles something incoherent, and I do the first thing
that pops into my mind. I slip my mom's phone from her pocket,
dial 911, and run the hell out of the place.

• • •

The next morning it's all over the news:

FBI DIRECTOR KILLED BY DECAPITATOR.

Zach woke up, tied and blindfolded, and started yelling. The police traced the open 911 line and dispatched a unit. With my mom there, everyone assumed she had tried to rescue my friend and saw her own death come out of it. Zach couldn't confirm or deny it. All he remembers is waking up, not how he got there, or what happened.

My mom's a hero.

Five days later at the funeral filled with mostly FBI, I stand with my family and receive hugs from people I don't even know. Why is it that people feel that hugging is the right thing to do to a perfect stranger upon death?

I'm not sure what I want, but it's not all these hugs.

Beside me stands my sister, close enough to touch me, but not entirely there. She doesn't know that I know she's slept at the foot of my bed every night this week. And that's okay.

Slightly behind me hovers Reggie, who has been completely shell-shocked over the whole thing. She loved my mom, as did everyone. Reggie's convinced she holds fault in all this. She gave me the Maryland address that I "passed" along to my mom. The same address my mom and Zach were found at.

I've kept so much from Reggie. So much I'll never tell. All I can do is reassure her she's not to blame in any way.

Victor and Justin are to my left. Justin has been glued to his dad's side, and I only hope this doesn't majorly mess my brother up. Surprisingly, Victor seems to be handling things well. Efficiently. Like the task-oriented person he is. I imagine in private, though, he gives in to the emotion of having lost his wife. I'm ashamed to have ever thought he might have had something to do with all this.

I wonder how we'll all be a month from now. Six months from now. A year. We'll be different. I already am. Killing Mom has changed me. I'm not quite sure how yet, but it has. I'm different now.

Through the crowd I spot Zach and Dr. Issa. I look at Zach first, but he's not looking at me. His gaze is fixed on the ground. Emotionally he has been through a lot, and I hope he doesn't turn back to the alcohol abuse he'd used before as an escape.

I switch my glance to Dr. Issa, who smiles gently and nods. That smile, that nod, *that's* what I need.

Someone hiccups a sob, and I glance to the right where a woman stands gazing at my mom's oversize portrait. I take in the portrait, the woman sobbing, and all the other people in the room.

Paperwork on my fake uncle popped up, stating his body had been found in Mexico. It's paperwork, I imagine, my mom coordinated weeks ago to "solve" the case. The FBI officially announced that the Decapitator and my uncle were one and the same and that he picked Zach as his first victim in a new planned spree. That he was going to switch from preschool teachers to teenage boys. A few serial killers in the past have switched "tastes," so the FBI's explanation is plausible.

Everyone *knows* I'm not to blame, but they can't hide their looks and whispers that I'm related to the infamous Decapitator and that because of Zach's friendship with me, he was targeted and taken. They can say what they want.

I haven't been back to school yet, but I imagine when I do, I'm going to get the fallout from all this. Eventually it will blow over as everything does. I only hope Zach and I can get back to some sort of friendship. Even if it's just polite nodding.

I searched my mom's office for all the stuff she'd taken from me and never given to the FBI. The flash drive, the envelopes, the message log . . . I found them and disposed of all the evidence.

Yes, everyone thinks the Decapitator is dead. To them and to my family my mom's a hero. And that's the way it's going to be. No one will ever know the truth.

Acknowledgments

Tim Carter, Sam Morton, and Megan Records: Thank you for being my first readers. Without your critique, insight, and suggestions, this book would definitely not be the sharp read that it is. Also, Tim, thank you for playing out the fight scenes with me, for your research talents, but most importantly—for your never-ending support.

Jenny Bent and Gemma Cooper: I don't even know where to start. A HUGE thank-you for all the rounds we did on getting this manuscript into top-notch shape. Your vision and unending patience turned this angry book into one badass novel.

Patrick Price: I'm so happy to be working with you. Bless you for seeing the appeal and snatching this project up. Really, seriously, thank you for that!

Simon Pulse family: Mara Anastas, Paul Crichton, Michelle Fadlalla, Anna McKean, Jessica Handelman, Katherine Devendorf, Julie Doebler, Emma Sector, and Carolyn Swerdloff. You are all a truly amazing force. I am so honored to be working with you.

Simone Elkeles: We go back a long way, my friend. . . . I greatly appreciate your business mind, your bluntness, and your willingness to "talk me off the ledge." I'm so glad I listen to you!

Finally, to all my online friends and followers: You really do make my day! You can find me at www.segreen.net, on Twitter @Shan_E_Green, and on my Facebook fan page under S. E. Green.

About the Author

S. E. Green calls North Florida home. *Killer Instinct* is her debut young adult thriller. Find her at www.segreen.net, on Twitter at @Shan_E_Green, or on her Facebook fan page.